The Comatose Cat

*Also by Sandy Dengler
in Large Print:*

A Model Murder
Murder on the Mount

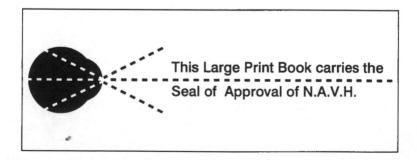

This Large Print Book carries the
Seal of Approval of N.A.V.H.

CHURCH CHOIR
MYSTERIES™

The
Comatose
Cat

Sandy Dengler

Thorndike Press • Waterville, Maine

Thomson Gale 27.95 12/05

Published in 2004 by arrangement with Guideposts Book Division.

Thorndike Press® Large Print Christian Mystery.

The tree indicium is a trademark of Thorndike Press.

The text of this Large Print edition is unabridged.
Other aspects of the book may vary from the original edition.

Set in 16 pt. Plantin by Liana M. Walker.

Printed in the United States on permanent paper.

Library of Congress Cataloging-in-Publication Data

Dengler, Sandy.
    The comatose cat
        p. cm. — (Church choir mysteries)
    ISBN 0-7862-6063-7 (lg. print : hc : alk. paper)
    1. Women detectives — Fiction. 2. Church musicians —
Fiction. 3. Choirs (Music) — Fiction. 4. Cats —
Fiction. 5. Large type books. I. Title. II. Series.
PS3554.E524C66 2004
    813'.54—dc22   2003061360

For cats,
and the lucky people upon whom
they deign to lavish their affections.

As the Founder/CEO of NAVH, the only national health agency solely devoted to those who, although not totally blind, have an eye disease which could lead to serious visual impairment, I am pleased to recognize Thorndike Press* as one of the leading publishers in the large print field.

Founded in 1954 in San Francisco to prepare large print textbooks for partially seeing children, NAVH became the pioneer and standard setting agency in the preparation of large type.

Today, those publishers who meet our standards carry the prestigious "Seal of Approval" indicating high quality large print. We are delighted that Thorndike Press is one of the publishers whose titles meet these standards. We are also pleased to recognize the significant contribution Thorndike Press is making in this important and growing field.

Lorraine H. Marchi, L.H.D.
Founder/CEO
NAVH

* Thorndike Press encompasses the following imprints: Thorndike, Wheeler, Walker and Large Print Press.

1

"Let's get our music and get out there, people. Time's a-wasting!" Barb Jennings, Eternal Hope's choir director, was hastening her flock.

Gracie Parks would be the first to agree. Somehow, choir rehearsals never seemed to start on time, whether everyone arrived promptly or not. Probably, it was because the members all tended to talk instead of assemble, catching each other up on Willow Bend's latest rumblings and rumors. On the other hand, where else could you hear all the news without commercial interruption?

She leafed hurriedly through her box, mumbling. " 'Mighty Fortress.' Where are you?"

Impatiently, Barb asked, "Where's Don Delano?"

"Don's home nursing a cold. He sends his regrets." Lester Twomley slid his file of music out of its sleeve. "He called me this afternoon."

Estelle Livett, their Soprano Extraordinaire, announced to no one in particular, "Betty Lou's girl ran off again. I heard it from Louise Thayer. You know, the one with the pierced earring in her eyebrow."

Tish, one of the Turner twins, frowned. "Louise got her eyebrow pierced too?"

"No, no, no. Betty Lou's daughter."

Tish looked confused. "She already had one eyebrow pierced."

"Incidentally, everybody," short little Lester Twomley tapped his music on the door jamb for emphasis, "keep your head up and your foot off the gas if you're driving near Cherry Tree Road. I wouldn't call it a speed trap exactly, but they're ticketing drivers right and left. Two miles over the limit and whammo. They've got you."

Rick Harding chuckled. "What's the matter, Les? You get nabbed?"

"No, but Harry down at the gas station did. And the sub-contractor — the painter — what's his name? Roy. Roy Bell. I was sitting in the barber's yesterday afternoon, waiting for my haircut. Roy and Harry were in the chairs. They ranted and raved so constantly I got sick of listening to them. I cancelled my appointment and left. It wasn't as if they were falsely accused.

8

They were just mad about getting caught."

"I say, good!" Estelle nodded enthusiastically. "It's about time they crack down on those people who whip around the residential streets at fifty miles an hour. Someone's going to run over a child. Or a pet."

"Speaking of pets," Gracie paused in her search for *Mighty Fortress*. "Mrs. Benton's cat got sick — I mean, very ill. Mysteriously ill. He nearly died."

Marge Lawrence, her face framed this evening in an upswept tangle of curls, turned to stare. "Why, I know that cat. A big black tom that wanders all over the neighborhood." Marge was a dog person, but she reserved a soft spot in her heart, Gracie knew, for any small furry thing.

"That's the one. Does anyone have two copies of 'Mighty Fortress'? I can't find it in mine."

"People!" Barb cracked her whip — figuratively, of course. "To the choir loft! Let's go!"

Tish and Lester followed her out the door.

Gracie sighed. She'd just have to double up with someone else. She closed the vestry door behind her.

The group thundered somewhat as they climbed the back stairs to the loft. This

9

lovely church, a century old at least, tended to reverberate a lot. The stair steps needed re-setting, too. They creaked. Gracie lived in an older home. She knew the constant, loving attention old buildings require.

As the choir filed into their appointed places, the topic of conversation shifted away from speeders. Gracie listened to chatter about an agent of some sort who worked for developers of some sort, scouting the area to find a location for a factory of some sort. Or something like that. No one seemed actually to know anything.

"And another thing Don mentioned on the phone today. He says the Larson boy learned how to make guncotton with his chemistry set." Lester paused for dramatic effect as he took his place in the seat behind Estelle. "Blew the windows out of the Larsons' basement."

Impatiently, Barb tapped her baton, overlooking the appreciative snorts of those able to appreciate such youthful enthusiasm for scientific endeavor.

Gracie frowned suddenly. "What's that smell?"

Barb raised her baton. She lowered it as her nose wrinkled. Her eyes grew wide.

The odor intensified. Gracie hadn't smelled anything so noxious since the time she'd inadvertently broken a rotten egg while cooking a special meal for her husband. The resulting stench had forced a complete evacuation of the whole house, cat and all.

"Must be a gas leak!" Rick grabbed Lester's shoulder and yanked him to his feet. "Everybody! Out of here!"

Gracie stood up. "No, it's not gas. I know gas smell. This is something else."

Something worse.

Much worse.

In fact, horrible! It didn't just assault the nose, it irritated like an odorous sandpaper.

"Come on!" Marge pushed past her, running for the stairs.

Estelle made a mistake then. Taking a deep breath before moving toward the exit, she nearly collapsed, hacking and choking. Rick grabbed one of her arms and Lester the other. They hauled her forward as she gasped.

Gracie hurried for the stairs by herself. She felt very close to being sick.

Within a few brief moments, the erstwhile rehearsers stood in a knot on the darkening church lawn. The street light on the corner bathed them in its gray-green glow. The effect didn't help Gracie's queasiness one bit.

Estelle, the hardest hit of them, sprawled

on the grass, obviously wretched. Gracie sat down next to her, sucking in deep draughts of cool, clean evening air.

It was hard to remember how peacefully the evening had begun.

Gracie drove her trusted Cadillac, Fannie May, home, thinking of the events of the evening. *God*, she started saying aloud, *I hope You'll help us get rid of that smell and make sure no one gets sick. We need to practice to better sing Your praise. Let me know if I can be useful. Thanks and Amen*. She felt better already.

2

In all his feline majesty, Gooseberry the cat draped himself across the back of the over-stuffed chair by the kitchen door. With the haughtiness to which only the truly regal can aspire, he watched his mistress and her companion busy themselves around the kitchen table. His pumpkin color complemented the chair's brown nicely; his white feet contrasted with it. And the black stripes did nothing to camouflage him. Gracie had read once that tigers' stripes help them hide in grass. She never did quite understand how that worked, being the owner of His Gaudiness. Stripes didn't hide Gooseberry from a solitary thing.

"How old is Jeffrey, anyway?" Gracie asked. She was catering his birthday party with the help of her neighbor, Marge Lawrence. And now they were completing the final details before delivery.

"Fourteen, but Jessica says don't put the number on the cake. He likes to think he's older."

Uncle Miltie, sitting nearby and watching them, laughed. He'd come to live with his widowed niece after his wife had died, and he knew he would soon enjoy the left-behinds and left-overs. He said, "The children want to be older, and the oldsters want to be younger. Go figure."

On the cake top, Gracie adjusted the little glass flask to a picturesque tilt. "This is the first time I ever used chemistry equipment to decorate a cake."

Marge cocked her head critically. "Doesn't look bad at all, actually. In fact, it's very festive. It's certainly different."

"Jeffrey is different."

"Now that's a true story!" Marge stretched plastic wrap across the deviled-egg tray and snugged it down. "He's either going to win the Nobel Prize or blow up Willow Bend."

Gracie grinned. "Maybe both." She glanced toward Gooseberry. Would the cat follow them today, as he sometimes did? Or was he in a lazy phase just now?

Lazy phase, apparently. With utter disdain, he watched them carry the ice cream, cake and snack trays out the back door to Marge's van. Though, like Uncle Miltie, he often snacked on bowls of rum raisin and butter pecan. Gracie took one last glance at him as she closed the door behind her. Those glowing eyes were drifting shut. Uncle Miltie's, too, looked tired from all the effort of watching. But he managed a good-luck wave.

It took less than ten minutes to drive from Gracie's house to the Larsons', but then, just about everywhere in Willow Bend was close to everywhere else. Marge pulled into the elegant curved driveway beside the house. One of the larger residences in Willow Bend, the Larson home sprawled picturesquely behind its circular driveway and professionally landscaped front yard.

Gracie, her arms full, headed for the front door. Suddenly, Roy Bell's head popped up out of the bushes by the foundation. At full stature, the man was only five-six or so. Hunkered in the shrubbery like that, he looked like a leprechaun in denim overalls. His half-bald head bobbed.

She smiled. "Why, hello, Roy! What are you doing down there?"

"Glazing their basement windows. How's that cat-monster of yours doing?"

"Now, Roy. As I said so many times, Gooseberry didn't mean to startle you like that. He sometimes just likes to make dramatic entrances."

"Startled!" Roy was indignant. "Scared

the living daylights out of me. Next time I come over there to do some work for you, I'll expect you to lock him up in a closet or something. Don't like things coming out of nowhere and pouncing on me like that."

"Don't worry. I will." Gracie, shifting the tray she was carrying, freed a hand to knock.

Jessica Larson swung the door open and stepped aside. Tall and graceful, she would have been a more attractive woman, Gracie thought, if only she would smile. "Come in, Gracie! The cake will go over there on that table, but we'll serve the finger foods from the sideboard in the dining room." Instantly, her demeanor snapped from cheerful to angry. "Rocky Gravino! Are you still here?" She glared at the front door behind Gracie.

Gracie turned around to look at the editor and publisher of the *Mason County Gazette*. His burly form filled the doorway, his shock of salt and pepper hair backlighted by the afternoon sun behind him. "Just trying to establish some facts, Jessica."

"Well, establish them somewhere else! I insist that you leave immediately."

Rocky looked at Gracie. "Say, Gracie, you know everyone in Mason County. Do you know a farmer named Billingsly?"

"Frank? Why, yes."

"Talk to him lately?"

"Enough!" Jessica snapped imperiously. "Get out!"

From somewhere behind Rocky, Marge called, "Excuse me," and pushed past Rocky with the punch buckets. She glanced quizzically at Gracie. Gracie sent the barest of confused looks back.

"Hello, Rocky." Marge headed for the refreshment table with her load.

"No, Marge, not there," ordered Jessica. "I want the punch in the kitchen. Drips, you know." Jessica directed her off beyond swinging doors, following behind her, talking like an auctioneer with a time limit. Jessica seemed to have every minute detail worked out. Gracie just hoped she had some plan for when a birthday reveler spilled not a drip of punch but a whole glass.

Rocky stepped in beside Gracie. "Frank and his family didn't feel so great, themselves, at about the same time he lost nearly half of his flock of sheep. Crazy, huh?"

"But I don't see how I could possibly help. . . ."

"Gracie, you never pry and you don't gossip, but somehow you always seem to know what's going on. It could be you know something helpful but you don't know that you know it, know what I mean?"

17

Frankly, she wasn't sure, but she let it go. "I'll tell you what. Why don't you —"

Jessica came storming into the living room. "Out! I told you."

The newspaper editor raised both hands. "I'm gone, Jessica." He turned on his heel and left, and in the process very nearly ran into a boy of twelve or thirteen. Gracie knew most of the children in town, but she didn't know this one. He looked undersized and over-tousled and had a waif-like quality.

He looked warily at Jessica.

She frowned. "Roger, what are you doing here? The party isn't for an hour."

"Mom had to send me here early."

She sighed. "Very well. Jeffy is in the back."

Despite the interesting little scene between Rocky and Jessica, Gracie had work to do. She hurried outside to the van.

Rocky had been sidetracked. Rather, he had been stopped in his tracks, because Marge was carrying a tray of deviled eggs and other hors d'oeuvres past him. He eyed the morsels with more than casual interest as they went by.

Gracie paused. "We only deliver the perfect ones to our clients. The brokers are still in my kitchen. But they taste just as good. Come by my house in an hour or so, and you can help us use them up."

He looked pleased. "Wouldn't want to waste. I'll forget to worry about cholesterol."

"Of course not." She watched him compress himself into his tiny black sedan. Who knows? She might even find out what was going on here. Why was Jessica so defensive? Why would Rocky come here to the Larsons' at all? Jessica was a perpetual civic volunteer and her husband owned a body shop and insurance agency. What would that have to do with dead sheep?

Gracie scooped up the cake, the centerpiece of the party, and carried it carefully up the steps and in the door. She stopped because Jessica stood between her and the table.

"Gracie, you are not to say a thing to that man! Not a word! I mean it!"

Gently, Marge moved Jessica aside. Gracie continued to the table and just in time. Her arms were getting tired. For a moment, she felt indignant. What nerve of Jessica, to think she could tell Gracie whom and whom not to talk to!

Fie, Gracie. Be charitable! She's flustered and hurried and just not thinking. Jessica was Jessica, always in control — or else attempting to be. Gracie would not prolong the situation by saying anything aloud, but to herself, quickly, she forgave Jessica her difficult nature.

Marge brought in the last of their carefully packed containers and stuffed the ice cream in the freezer. Gracie stepped back from the sideboard to admire their work.

Jessica was explaining: "There's an accessory kit to Jeffy's chemistry set that children twelve and under aren't allowed to buy. We got that for him years ago, of course, when he was nine or ten. He was ready for it. Now he's fascinated with computers. That's where the big money is, you know. Computers! Computers and chemistry. And he is so precocious at both."

Gracie laid a hand on Marge's arm. "We must be going. Much to do yet."

"Oh, absolutely!" Marge thrust a roll of oversized plastic bags into Jessica's hands. "Now you just stuff the trays and everything into sacks and we'll be by later to pick them up."

Gracie frowned. "Jessica? What's that strange noise?"

"Oh, good!" the mother replied. "He got it flying! Listen!"

"Got what flying?" Marge glanced nervously about. "It sounds like something in the hall."

"Jeffy invented a computer-controlled helicopter! Isn't that wonderful? All by himself! He designed it, made the propellant himself, everything! He is such an amazing child!"

Wonderful was not exactly the word Gracie would have used. Sure enough, a white helicopter about a foot long came chirring out into the living room, four feet off the floor. It looked like a dragonfly with a racing stripe. Tilting, it traced a sinuous S curve around the room. Marge had to duck quickly to avoid being chopped by the rotors.

Its whine suddenly grew rougher. It sputtered and coughed, wagging slightly. Then, straight as an arrow, the noisy little monster zoomed across the room and splooched nose-first into the birthday cake.

3

"As I always say," Marge crowed, "the quickest way to a man's heart is through the soft underbelly." She pointed toward Rocky Gravino's little sedan parked in front of Gracie's house. She wheeled her van into Gracie's driveway.

As Gracie slid out, she thought to herself, *Actually, I think it was Walt Kelly who said that in his comic strip.* Her husband El had been a lifelong Pogo fan. How she missed the man.

Rocky got out of his car and started up the walk. By the time Gracie had unlocked her door, he was hovering over her shoulder.

Marge and Rocky followed her inside.

The door closed.

As one, the women turned on him.

"What in the world did you say to Jessica to get her so upset?" Marge demanded as Gracie asked, "Why in heaven's name did you go there about dead sheep?"

He looked at them. "Are the broken ones

really as good as the others?"

What could she do? Gracie had just encountered an irresistible force. She led them all to the kitchen and waved toward a chair. Rocky sat, Marge started a pot of coffee, and Gracie got out the big glass bowl of leftovers and broken ends. She also set before her male guest some flatware and a napkin, the last of the homemade bread, and a jar of strawberry jam.

For some reason, this afternoon Gooseberry had abandoned the chair for the top of the refrigerator. His tail and hind leg draped down in front of the freezer section. He did not move, either, when Gracie opened the refrigerator door.

Marge plunked three coffee mugs down on the table. "Start talking, pal. This is no free lunch."

He watched Gracie cut a generous slab of bread. "Marge, do you know Frank Billingsly?"

"His wife visits her parents in Florida every winter for three months, his son plays junior varsity soccer, and his oldest daughter is dating that Moon boy with the green hair." Marge put out milk and sugar. "No. Why?"

Rocky looked at Gracie.

She thought about it a moment. "He's a

very well organized and thoughtful man. For example, late every winter he calls around to his regular customers, you might say. We tell him if we want our gardens roto-tilled. Then he picks a day when the ground is dry enough and brings in that little putt-putt tractor of his. He does all our gardens at once."

"Not the kind to be careless."

"Oh, my, no." Gracie sat down and pulled a mug toward her. "Except for having my garden dug, I almost never see him, now that he doesn't raise chickens anymore. He used to sell me fertile eggs when he was sup-plying chicks to the hatcheries."

Rocky grunted, but his attention had been diverted by that first sweet bite of bread and homemade jam. For a few moments, he simply stared off into space, or maybe he was only pondering Gracie's souvenir velvet dice from Las Vegas. They did stick out rather prominently by the refrigerator.

Marge slid into a chair. "Come on, Gravino. Talk."

"I didn't know about the soccer. I did hear his son is also on the JV track and cross-country teams. The boy was out of town at a meet. He didn't get sick. The three Billingslys at home got what seemed like ptomaine with a headache. They didn't go

24

to a doctor, figuring it was food poisoning."

"In other words, the boy didn't eat what they did."

"Actually, he did. They all had breakfast together and then he got on the athletic bus. Eight hours later, whammo — them, but not him."

Gracie nodded. "Eight to ten hours after eating contaminated food is when food poisoning occurs. What about the sheep?"

"About the same time all this is happening, Frank discovers his sheep are dropping over in their pasture. Some sick, some dead. No one knows why."

"What does the veterinarian say?" Marge poured coffee.

"Hasn't a clue."

"How about the county extension agent?" Gracie watched Rocky pick some morsels from the leftovers bowl.

"Her either. She suggested maybe someone dumped antifreeze along the road and the sheep picked it up while they were grazing."

"Antifreeze?" Marge wrinkled her nose.

"Antifreeze is deadly poison for animals. You drain your radiator and let the stuff run into the ditch, you're just inviting some cute little furry critter to drop dead. It's not only poisonous. It's also attractively tasty to some animals."

Kind of like broken hors d'oeuvres are to editors, Gracie mused to herself. She continued her musings aloud. "One of the reasons you stopped by Larsons' was that he runs an auto shop? Because you thought Ed Larson might be dumping used antifreeze?"

"Possibility. Then there's that weird kid. Jeffrey. Him and that chemistry set of his. What if he's practicing toward the day when he'll make his debut as a mass murderer by poisoning the city water supply? Did you see him? His eyebrows are burnt off."

"Not surprising." Marge grimaced. "No, we didn't see him. We were too busy ducking his latest invention."

"The helicopter?" Rocky grinned. "Yeah. He demonstrated it for me. He has every room in his house mapped out on his computer. The chopper shows up on his screen as a red dot. He directs the bird from his room, with a joystick. Flies it all over the house without hitting anything, based on the computerized map. Quite an invention, when you think about it."

Marge merely sniffed.

Gracie shook her head. "Unless you get your radiator drained and filled at a shop or service station, you can't easily dispose of used antifreeze. Because of all those new environmental laws. Rocky, anyone could dump it where Frank's sheep might find it. How many high school boys are going to go to the hazardous waste facility to dispose of something they can pour into a ditch after dark? Or anyone else who can't or won't be bothered?"

Rocky nodded. "Another funny thing. Old Pete Murphy's dog died suddenly a couple days ago. Only four years old. Pete came into the office to see if we could run an obit."

"On the dog?!" Marge stared.

"Favorite dog, apparently."

Gracie felt the need to point out, "Marge, if Charlotte died, you'd be at the editorial office when they opened, obituary in hand."

"Charlotte's *different*."

Rocky plucked another broker out of the bowl. "Say, what's this about a stink bomb in your church?"

Gracie frowned at Marge.

Marge wagged her head. "Stink, yes. Bomb, no. We never did find out what it was."

"So that's the official line, huh?"

"Rocky." Gracie tried an egg herself, though normally she didn't nibble. "Who would stink-bomb a church on a weekday evening?"

"That's also got my curiosity working," Rocky said. "If you're going to pull that particular prank, why not do it on Sunday for maximum effect?"

They talked on, enjoying each other's familiar company, but their conversation offered nothing more of substance. With satisfied thanks, Rocky eventually excused himself and Gracie saw him to the door. She glanced at the clock as she wandered back to the kitchen. They should leave to go clean up at the Larsons' soon.

Gooseberry leaped from the refrigerator to the floor with a loud thump and strolled in his stately manner toward the dining room.

Marge remained at the table, staring at her mug of cold coffee.

Gracie opened her mouth to speak, then closed it again. She sat down beside Marge. "What's wrong?"

Marge shook her head. "Nothing."

Gracie knew Marge couldn't stand silence, so she simply said nothing. The ploy worked in less than twenty seconds.

"Gracie, I knew Pete's dog. Young and healthy. A great little guy. So lively." Marge looked into her friend's eyes. "What if some disease is going around no one knows about? A sort of canine Ebola,

28

you know? Frank's family gets sick. His sheep die. The dog dies. It frightens me. What if my Charlotte got sick, Gracie? She's so delicate."

"Please don't worry, Marge. Shih Tzus look delicate, but they're remarkably tough. You know that. And Charlotte doesn't run free."

"No, but she goes where other dogs go."

Gracie drew a deep breath. She laid her hand on Marge's.

"How often have you heard, 'it never rains but what it pours'? In fact, you yourself say it frequently. Things do happen in bunches. And then we notice them more only because they did clump together instead of being spread out more evenly. We see patterns where there are none, really."

Marge looked at her. "That's true. Remember the dented fender plague last winter? Rocky even commented on it in his editorial column. A rash of dented fenders, and it seemed as if it must have been intentional, or else contagious!"

"Only because his was one of the fenders that got dented. If I hear anything about any other dogs, I'll let you know, of course."

"I know." Marge straightened and smiled. "You're right about things happening in bunches. Odd coincidence."

"That's the phrase. Odd coincidence." But, somehow, very deep down inside, Gracie herself was not so sure.

4

"You can catch more flies with honey than with vinegar, but a fly-swatter's still your best bet." Frank Billingsly, farmer, sage and historian, frequently waxed philosophical. But rarely did his philosophizing match up to whatever the conversational topic happened to be at the moment. It did not do so now.

A bit of grey stubble peeked out from under his baseball cap. Gracie could never remember him without his cap, except in church. And that was only when his wife, with a sharp elbow, reminded him to take it off. He leaned now on the fender of his battered old pickup truck as he gazed out across Gracie's lawn toward Marge's house. He looked at her, blinking cheerfully. "So how's your catering business coming, Gracie?"

She leaned back against his fender. "On again, off again, but I do miss your good eggs. They were richer than store-bought, and much fresher. When you broke one of those into the pan, the yolk stood right up there."

Stacked in the bed of Frank's pickup were a dozen wooden crates stuffed full of chickens of various colors and sizes. They were clucking disapprovingly. Wads of feathers pressed against the crates' wooden bars and occasionally drifted free through the slats.

Frank nodded. "Free-range hens always lay better eggs. I'm more than ready to go back to raising chickens. Sheep are a pain in the wool knickers."

"I understand you lost some. That must have been a difficult setback."

"Actually, they were insured. A setback though, as you say. Sheep are supposed to be good for a farmer. They thrive on poorer pasture than cows can. They don't need much supplemental feed. And every year you get a crop of wool and two crops of lambs. But, gosh, are they ever stupid! Stupider even than chickens. They make mushrooms look smart."

Gracie smiled. "You always did do well with chickens."

"True. But only half of the work with these birds is re-establishing a flock. Now I have to round up enough customers again to make it worth my while. The big super-markets, they don't buy local free-range eggs."

"Count me as a customer. And I'll probably use five or six dozen a week more eggs now than I used to."

Frank was standing with his back to the world. Gracie, however, was facing the street. So she noticed first the gawky, gangling young man, high school age or thereabouts, who was lurking up by the corner, watching them. In fact, lurking was putting it mildly. The boy was studying them with binoculars. And although her eyes weren't good enough to discern facial features at that distance, it didn't matter. She knew who it was. Only one person in Willow Bend dyed his hair bright green.

Chuckie Moon.

"Frank? I understand your daughter is interested in Thelma Moon's son."

"Yeah, he shows up now and then. Never when you need him or there's work to do. I figure if a young man is serious about a girl, he should be willing to lend a hand now and then. Like Jacob, for instance, in Genesis, who worked for his future father-in-law seven years for Rachel. He ended up with Leah, so he worked another seven years. Now that's serious intentions. I realize there's some folks who would criticize him for sticking it to his brother Esau, but you can't fault him as a son-in-law."

Gracie was all set to point to the street corner and say, "Why, look! Isn't that he?" But when she glanced that way, the boy was gone. Questions flooded into her mind. Why had he been there to start with? How had he disappeared so quickly? And although his intent obviously was to spy, weren't binoculars just a wee bit blatant?

"On the other hand," Frank rolled on, oblivious to the world, "he carted Laban's daughters off without a by-your-leave, so I suppose no one's perfect." Lurching erect, he undraped himself from his truck and drew a deep breath. "Well, guess I'll head on. Got about six others I want to talk to yet. I'll call you in a couple days, set up a schedule."

"Very good. Thank you, Frank."

Seemingly in no hurry whatever, Frank slowly climbed in. His little pickup's motor coughed, then roared. It sounded about the way the battered old vehicle looked. The hood vibrated. With his chickens still voicing their complaints, he drove away down the street.

Curiosity got the better of her. Instead of

going back into the house, Gracie took a walk to the corner. She continued around the block but caught no glimpse of green hair, not that she particularly expected to. Chuckie had seen her looking at him. He would surely leave quickly and not hang around to be spotted a second time.

On impulse, she cut back through the alley toward her backyard. It was, she knew, Gooseberry's habit of entry, his favorite way to come home.

And there he was. Not Gooseberry. Chuckie. He was sitting in a very small car with his back to her and did not seem inclined to check his rearview mirror while parked in an alley. He obviously did not see her as she walked up behind him.

"You're Charles Moon, aren't you?" Gracie's voice sent him a foot straight up. He apparently didn't use a seat belt when he was parked, either.

He glanced at her briefly. "Yes, ma'am. Gotta go now."

You won't learn answers if you don't ask questions, so Gracie went right ahead and inquired straight out what she wanted to learn. "I noticed you up on the corner with binoculars. Are you a birder? You know, one of those people who watch birds?"

"No, ma'am." And then his face brightened and he actually met her eye. "I was looking at your car in your driveway. It's shiny. I'm working on mine, and I was wondering what you use to get your car so shiny."

"Coke and baby wipes."

For a second his demeanor seemed to switch from bright to furious. The change — so complete and so rapid — was almost frightening. It was certainly mysterious.

"You don't believe me, but it's true," she said to him, ignoring his glance. "Bring your car around to the front of my house and I'll show you." She continued down the alley to enter her yard by the back gate.

Would he follow or would he drive away? She didn't exactly care. She wouldn't mind a bit if he disappeared — not the way his mood changed so radically — but she got a can of Coke, some paper towels and baby wipes and went out front anyway.

Here he came. He pulled into her drive behind her car and got out very cautiously.

She popped the top and poured from the can onto a towel. "Many soft drinks contain citric acid and usually some other helpful ingredients as well. The acid cuts rust." She demonstrated the cleaning properties of her system on his chrome-plated front bumper. "I just happen to be using Coke because it's what I had in the house. Experiment with different soft drink products. See what works best for you."

She then went over his bumper with a baby wipe. "These things are wonderful for lots of uses. I polish my bathroom fixtures with one. Makes them absolutely glow." She tactfully neglected to mention that her bathroom then smelled rather like a diaper and so would Chuckie's bumper when she was done. She stood up and nodded, satisfied.

Chuckie's bumper looked almost new. Well, maybe not that good, but not bad at all.

Gracie gave him the opened Coke can. "It will take more than one pass to get rid of all the rust, but you can see that we already cleaned off a lot of the little spots." She handed her nearly empty box of baby wipes to him. "You may have this. Try them on your dashboard and upholstery, too."

He mumbled something that probably was some sort of thanks. He also looked confused, as if he were not sure how he had suddenly ended up with a box of baby wipes in his hand.

Gracie almost opened the car door for

him, thought that might be a bit pushy, and waited.

As it turned out, he did not require the hint. He jumped in and cranked the ignition, then backed out and drove away.

It was only as Gracie watched him go that she realized an alarming fact: He had frightened her.

5

Gracie did not revel in the joy of shopping nearly as much as did Marge or Estelle, but she did love to shop at Miller's. If you kept an animal, any animal, Miller's Feed Store sold what you needed. Whether it was the igloo-shaped doghouses stacked in one corner, the saddles and curry combs, or the martin houses stacked in the other, Miller's offered it all. And to Gracie, what felt homiest and most old-fashioned was the dust that lay over everything.

This morning, Gracie was shopping for cat food, litter and a new toy for Gooseberry. She stepped from bright morning sun into the gloom of the ancient showroom with its incandescent lighting and too few windows that were too infrequently washed.

A gaggle of overalls-clad gentlemen at rest sat on the benches beside the counter. Gracie recognized Harry Durant and Roy Bell, but the names of the remaining three escaped her.

"H'lo, Gracie." Harry Durant's voice sounded like marbles in a blender. Harry folded his arms across his overalls bib, resting them on the ample paunch. He owned and operated a gas station, and always smelled vaguely of diesel fumes. Fortunately, he did not smoke.

"Good morning, Harry! Hello, Roy." She smiled at the three other men.

Roy Bell, the leprechaun-like contractor who glazed basement windows and did other handyman jobs, helloed her back.

"Good morning, Hammie." She nodded to the young man behind the counter. Hammie Miller grinned at her. His wife still had not gotten him to replace the front incisor he'd lost. He claimed, Gracie had heard, that unless it was corn-on-the-cob season, he didn't need that tooth, and when it was corn season, he couldn't handle the roasting ear with a false tooth anyway. So why go to the expense? Hammie prided himself on his logic and common sense.

Gracie mentally went down her shopping list — mentally, because the list itself lay forgotten on her kitchen counter. She ignored the aisle with the wormers, vitamins and other veterinary supplies and passed up the bird and hamster sections. She paused, though, at the cow aisle. Come to think of it, her supply of bag balm was getting low. She picked up a can and blew the dust off it.

Someone in the next aisle sneezed.

"Gesundheit!" She continued on to cats.

Behind her, Harry Durant inveighed mightily against the proposed factory coming to town. It was a curious stance for the owner of a gas station to take. Gracie thought surely his business would profit from workers driving around, but Harry had nothing nice to say about the prospect of manufacturing in Willow Bend.

Harry fumed, "Don't know who invited the scout to come looking, but I bet it was that nosy pastor over at Eternal Hope church."

Instantly, Gracie was all ears. Her church! He was talking about her Pastor Paul and her church.

Roy muttered something.

"Wouldn't put it past him." Harry fulminated. "He's always meddling. Sticking his nose in. Oughta just preach and visit the sick and quit making everybody else's business his business. Remember the time he told Mac Medline to quit drinking? Wasn't his place to say that."

"That company ain't just scouting, either." One of the other fellows chimed in. "I hear they're applying for the permits already."

Gracie scooped up a bag of litter and

41

headed back out toward the front.

"Nonsense!" Another voice. "They haven't for sure found a site yet. They're still considering that twenty acres along the creek near Frank Billingsly's. I saw the scout out there looking around, just a couple days ago. Last I heard, though, Frank wasn't amenable to selling."

Gracie put her purchases on the counter. A little cloud of dust flew up, then settled again.

"Hey, speaking of Frank," Roy Bell said, "his girl is taking up with Chuckie Moon."

"Chuckie Moon? The screwball with green hair?"

"Ah, he's not so bad." Roy stretched his short legs out. "I hire him now and then for roofing work. Ain't exactly the kind of kid Frank'd want for a son-in-law though."

"Will that be all today?" Hammie Miller poked at his iron-and-brass cash register.

Gracie dug into her purse. "And a carton of popcorn."

"George?" Hammie bellowed. "Fetch Gracie out a box of popcorn. It's on the far wall by the puppy chow." The cash register went ching.

One of the men on the benches got up and ambled through the double doors into the back room.

Gracie thought it over, and asked, even though she knew the answer, "the popcorn is next to the puppy chow?"

"I shelve the boxed stuff alphabetically." Hammie counted out the change into her hand.

Roy Bell now shifted the subject from the factory to speed traps. "It used to be on Cherry Tree Road," Roy griped, "but they've been moving it around. This morning they hauled me over clear out on Woodward! Third ticket this week! There ought to be a law against that kind of thing. Bad business, stopping people when they got work to do."

Gracie paused by the benches. "Roy? Has it occurred to you that if you observe the speed limit, they won't stop you?"

Harry cackled.

And Gracie realized instantly that her comment would have better been left unspoken, for now Roy really seemed irate.

She glanced at the dusty clock beyond the bird feeder display. "Oh, my! I have to hurry! Good-bye, gentlemen!"

By the time she got out the door, the conversation had already switched back to the factory again.

"Just what is it this factory's supposed to make?" Hammie's voice asked.

And as the door closed, the man named George was saying, "Near as I can figure out, according to Harry here, their main product's gonna be toxic waste."

Gracie sighed as she started up Fannie May, wishing she could do something to dispel all this bad feeling. Maybe the opportunity would arise.

6

Choir practice in a little less than three hours. Gracie had better step on it! Just as she was adding the celery and onion to the cubed potatoes and carrots, the doorbell rang. Of course: Always when your hands are full, never when you're at ease.

Gracie adjusted the flame beneath her pot and hurried out to the front room. She swung open the door. "Pastor Paul! Come in."

In lieu of a hat, Paul Meyer doffed his bike helmet as he stepped inside. "Sorry to drop in without calling ahead. I don't have my cell phone with me. Good afternoon."

Gracie smiled. "Good afternoon. It's always been my policy that unannounced visitors take potluck. The house might be cleaned up or it might not be. But they're always welcome. Have you had lunch?"

"Yes, thank you, Gracie."

"Did you get enough dessert at lunch?"

He looked confused for a moment, then broke into a laugh.

"I take it that's a 'maybe not.' There's fresh apple pie. Would you like some?"

"I can't turn it down."

"Neither can I. I think I'll join you. Milk or coffee?" Gracie led the way to the kitchen. For some reason, this tall, energetic young man invited mothering. He didn't mean to, Gracie was certain. But his sandy hair and soft facial features gave him a boyish appeal. Perhaps it was also that, although he was engaged, he technically had no woman to take care of him.

"Milk, please." Pastor Paul settled himself at the kitchen table and stuffed his helmet under his chair. "Have you heard that a factory might be coming to town?"

"Nothing but." Gracie set out two tumblers, two napkins and two forks and put the pie on the table. "For example, Harry Durant's negative attitude surprises me. Surely his business would benefit from new people coming in."

"Not necessarily." The pastor eyed the pie appreciatively. "I'm sure Harry knows the truth, but he doesn't want people to think he does. It would sound like he's just trying to kill the competition."

"Competition? Harry Durant operates a gas pump." Gracie poured the milk.

The pastor nodded. "The truth is, Gracie,

it's not just a factory. It's also a factory outlet. Auto parts and additives, and it will sell gas on the side."

Gracie cut a generous wedge and slipped it onto a dessert plate. "You're saying that the new plant will do just about everything Harry's gas station does." She handed the plate to Paul and cut herself a much smaller wedge.

"Well, a lot more besides. The company even plans to sign up locals to test experimental products they haven't placed on the market yet."

"That might be fun. It's too bad they don't make kitchen gadgets." She sat down and took a bite, and the minister followed her lead.

He smiled. "Oh, my! This pie is excellent. Just excellent. The new facility could be a godsend to this town."

"I know we've got too many high school graduates leaving the area who never return."

"Seventy percent have permanently left the county by the time they're twenty-five. Whether they go on to college or go directly into the work force, they can't stay. Our community college is a good one, but it doesn't offer enough. We don't have the higher education to keep our kids here, and we don't have the jobs. Especially since the shoe factory closed a few years ago."

"So that's why you are so strongly in favor of it."

The pastor nodded. "How many young families live on your block here right now?"

Gracie paused to mentally count neighbors. "The Hadlocks up on the corner have school-age children. They're the only ones. Oh, and the Griswolds." She frowned. "This is an older neighborhood, and the houses are old-fashioned, you might say. I just assumed that younger people would prefer being in a newer part of town. You know, two bathrooms in the house, fashionable modern design. I never thought about it."

"It's not only your older neighborhoods. It's the same story all over town. Willow Bend is losing the young people. And that is tomorrow's tax base."

Gracie paused to work a bite of pie over her tongue. She was her own toughest critic: It was a very good pie, yes, but it still needed a little something more to make it truly soar. "I noticed from the annual report that our church membership is dwindling."

"We discussed that very thing at the last regional pastors' breakfast. Everyone's is. And our churches have scores of young people who would prefer to stay near home if they could only support themselves." His milk glass was nearly empty.

Gracie got up for more milk. "Apart from Harry Durant and Roy Bell, is there much opposition?" She checked her soup pot. All was well.

"I don't think so. You have to remember that when the young people leave, the older generation is watching its children and grandchildren move away. So, many of them welcome development."

Gracie filled his glass again. "How about Frank Billingsly?"

"Oh, Frank isn't opposed to it as such. He just doesn't want them asphalting his family farm to build it. In other words, he's in favor of it, but in favor of it being somewhere else."

Gracie left the milk carton on the table on the considerable chance that it would be needed again, and sat down. "Do you think possibly the pie needs just a tad more of something?"

He shrugged. "Tastes perfect to me."

"Mmm. I can't think of a polite way to phrase my next question, so I'll simply ask it. Why did you stop by today?"

He chuckled. "To request a favor. Why else? You know just about everyone in town. In particular, you know most of the men and women on the town council."

"My husband was a councilman," she explained as she took another bite. Yes, it definitely needed something. What if she put just the tiniest dash of mace into her apple filling, to sharpen the other flavors? A wee pinch? "But you knew that."

"Exactly. The favor I'm asking of you is to help us put the idea of this factory before the public in the best way possible. You know people's needs, and you know the people themselves. Also, you don't have any vested interest in seeing it succeed or fail, so your opinion is objective."

"How would we go about it?" The additional spice would have to be very subtle, of course; not so much that the overall flavor would scream, mace! or nutmeg!

"I'd like to introduce you to the factory rep. You can decide from there whether or not to help. Also, do you have any suggestions about disarming the opposition?"

"Mace. Definitely, mace would do it."

Pastor Paul frowned. In fact, he looked shocked. "Wouldn't that be just a bit extreme?"

"A whiff. The barest bit. A suggestion only. Yes, that's it. Now about this company agent. Representative. Why did the company choose Willow Bend as a place to consider?"

The pastor smiled. "I invited them."

7

Don Delano was back. He adjusted his wire-rimmed glasses as he threaded among chairs. With gratitude, Gracie watched the cheery chemistry teacher take his place in the bass section. Without his strong baritone leading, the whole bass section tended to fade into the wallpaper.

Gracie sat down amid the altos.

Barb Jennings stepped up to the director's music stand. She said something, but everyone was shuffling sheet music; the pervasive rustling blotted out her words. Gracie rather assumed that her own hearing was to blame, mushing all noise together into one muffled sound, but her hearing certainly wasn't bad enough yet to waste time getting it checked. On the other hand, Amy Cantrell, seated in the soprano section directly in front of Gracie, seemed to hear perfectly well. She was digging out "Mighty Fortress." Amy was a pretty girl, and rather quiet.

On impulse, Gracie leaned forward. "Amy? Did you ever date Chuckie Moon?"

Amy twisted around to look at her. "Not Chuckie Green-Hair."

"What's wrong with him? — I mean, besides the chlorophyll where no chlorophyll should be."

Amy giggled. The smile fled as she thought a moment. "He's — I don't know how to describe it. When he gets angry, he gets nasty. He yells at people he shouldn't yell at and sometimes he throws things. He seems to really like figuring out some kind of revenge when he thinks someone was bad to him. I'm not explaining it well, but that's the way he is. I just stay away from him. Most of the kids do."

"But Frank Billingsly's daughter likes him, doesn't she?"

Amy shook her head. "She never wanted to go with him to start with, but he kind of pushed her into it. Now she wants to break up with him. She told me so. But he doesn't want to, you know? Guys never do unless they're the ones doing the breaking. The kids at school call him Up-Chuckie behind his back. Does that tell you anything?"

Barb cleared her throat with a cough that could be heard all the way to Chicago.

Amy untwisted and Gracie sat back straight.

Lester Twomley spoke up, voicing Gracie's own opinion. "We're not going to drag the tempo with 'Mighty Fortress' tonight, are we? It should sound like a triumph, not a funeral."

Estelle Livett turned to scowl at him. "A fortress, Lester, does not gallop. It must be stately!"

"But it's such poor form," Lester shot back, "when the congregation nods off while we're still singing."

"Stately, Lester."

"Your attention!" Barb rapped her baton against the music stand. She raised both hands, and —

Distant chimes played the opening bars of *Amazing Grace*.

"Cell phone. Sorry." Don Delano wasn't sorry enough to turn it off, though. His deep voice, still a bit husky from last week's cold, mumbled into it. He raised his voice. "Oh, yeah, sure, Uncle Miltie." Pause. "Uh huh. Riiight."

He frowned, then stood up. "Gracie? It's your Uncle Miltie. He says your Gooseberry is ill and lying on the mantel."

Choir members tittered.

"Oh, I forgot Uncle Miltie even knew

53

your cell phone number. He must have seen I left mine at home." Gracie reached to take the receiver from Don's hand.

Meanwhile, Barb attempted to restore order. "Well! He should know better than to interrupt a choir rehearsal for a cat. You'd think a man his age would exhibit better sense."

"He's becoming rather agitated." Don listened some more. "Here, Gracie, you take it."

Gracie listened intently. Something was definitely wrong. She stood up. "He does sound upset. I suppose I'd better go see what's happening. Thank you, Don. Barb, I'm sorry. I should go check it out."

"This rehearsal is important," Barb insisted, obviously putting cats a lot lower on her list of priorities.

"And you know I try never to miss any. I'll be back as soon as I can." Gracie grabbed her purse and headed for the stairs.

"I'm coming too! You might need someone to drive." Marge stayed close behind her, ignoring the choir director's protests.

Gracie knew that Marge, good-hearted though she was, was offering to help as much out of curiosity as charity. Her friend's sense of curiosity — let's not call it nosiness! — was active twenty-four hours a day.

Gracie hurried across the parking lot, digging for keys as she ran. Running and pawing through a purse are incompatible. She stopped for a second, found her keys, and thumbed the lock remote. Her concern was growing. Besides, she wanted to get this over with and return to the church quickly.

She was backing out even before Marge got her door closed. "Uncle Miltie is fussy, and his judgment isn't the best, but he isn't the kind to worry over nothing." Her car leaped forward. "And I can't imagine he'd think of that little detail about Gooseberry on the mantel. Despite liking high places, the Goose never climbs up on the mantel."

Marge's voice trembled. "And with all these mysterious illnesses and animal deaths and such . . . " Her words trailed off. She had just voiced the other reason for Gracie's concern.

Gracie would take Highland Boulevard. It wasn't shorter, but with fewer lights, it would be faster. She turned right and out onto the street. Also, the speed limit on Highland was forty-five as opposed to twenty-five on the more direct route. She would adhere scrupulously to speed limits, with the ticket-happy enforcers Lester

Twomley had mentioned lurking heaven-knows-where. A speeding ticket takes twelve minutes. She could not afford twelve minutes.

Marge teased her, "Are you sure that a woman your age should have burned rubber like that?"

Uncle Miltie, his spirit vastly larger than his eighty-year-old physique, was standing on the front porch as Gracie pulled into her drive. For a moment he looked particularly frail as he stood there between the front porch posts, propped within his walker. He had turned on the porch light, though dusk had not yet thoroughly settled in.

"I was afraid you wouldn't come quickly enough," he said as his niece ran up the steps.

The room was dark and cool and very quiet. It took Gracie a second to adjust to the gloom. She turned on the light by the sofa.

"I pulled the drapes," said Uncle Miltie behind her. "I poked at him a little but he wouldn't respond. With this blamed arthritis, I couldn't reach up there to lift him down."

From the doorway, Marge gasped. "Oh, Gracie."

Limp as a yard of yarn, Gooseberry lay

draped along the mantel, his eyes closed, his tongue hanging out. That magnificent tail dangled listlessly.

Reaching high, Gracie scooped him down and tucked him belly up in the crook of her arm. The cat smelled vaguely like . . . like something. She couldn't place the faint aroma, except that it was not any of the usual smells she'd detected on him from time to time. His head flopped out over her arm. Remarkably heavy it was, for the size of it. Oh, Gooseberry!

Wait. What was this?

Gracie laid her fingertips firmly along those fragile little ribs, all muffled in belly fur. Barely detectable, his chest vibrated. He wasn't purring audibly, but the purr was there.

For a moment, Gracie scratched his breastbone, his chin, his hard little head, lavishing affection upon her adored pet.

Her silly, haughty, drama-loving, histrionic cat.

Then she brought her lips close to his ear and whispered the magic words. "Tuna fish."

His neck muscles tightened, the head no longer lolling.

He lurched suddenly, arched his back into a C, and rolled over, dropping from her arm onto the carpet. He stretched, shook himself, and strode away to the kitchen.

Uncle Miltie blurted a few comments he usually reserved for skateboarders who cut him off in the park.

Marge, open-mouthed, muttered, "Why, I never!"

Gracie went out to the cupboard and found Gooseberry a treat. "Let's get back to choir practice."

Marge was still shaking her head as Gracie backed out into the street and headed off toward the church. "If that don't beat all! So he was faking."

"Maybe. But maybe not, at least not completely. He smells funny, as if he'd gotten into something. I think I'll recognize the odor if I come across it again. So he probably wasn't feeling well, but he certainly was nowhere near death's door."

"The door! He wasn't even near the building! Hey, why are you pulling over?" Marge glanced into the rearview mirror. "I don't believe it! That better not be Paulie Prince, the little scamp! I taught him piano when he was ten."

Flashing red, white and blue lights, hyperactive fireflies in the gathering dusk, loomed right behind them, commanding total attention.

Gracie shook her head. "I was under the limit! My lights are on, I don't think I cut anyone off, there aren't any stop signs to run . . . ."

The patrol car whipped past them. Its siren howled soft–loud–soft.

Her heart still pitter-patting, Gracie cautiously eased back into traffic and continued on.

"What's going on up there?" Marge rolled down her window and stuck her head out, craning to see ahead. Gracie made a mental note that Marge's dog Charlotte, the Shih Tzu, did exactly that same thing.

"The police station!" Gracie stopped because the patrol car, its lights still dancing, had stopped just ahead of her.

"Look at Gladys go!" Marge exclaimed.

A hundred feet ahead of them, Gladys Martin, the night dispatcher, came running out of the police station. She was covering her nose and mouth with the tail of her T-shirt. And right behind her came Herb Bowers, the chief. It was the fastest Gracie had ever seen him move.

Suddenly Marge pulled her head back in and rolled up her window. "Back up! Quick! Now! Turn into the parking lot right there!" She jabbed her finger toward the right. "You can get into the alley through it and over onto Third Street. Get out of here!"

For behind those two fleeing officers of the law, pouring out of the police station into the sweet night air, came that same horrible, penetrating stink that a week ago had cleared the Eternal Hope Church.

8

Ah, what a lovely day! Willow Bend smelled so nice in good weather like this. It was not any particular aroma that one could identify as such; it was simply the blended whole, just as a choir of voices melds together into a unified sound greater than its parts.

Gracie paused to turn off her Walkman. The tape had ended, and besides, she was getting nearer to the group of people milling around on the sidewalk up ahead, and she intended to stop and talk.

Much of the town was here, it seemed, rubber-necking. Clusters of people and curious kids loitered, paying casual attention to the police station up ahead.

She stopped alongside Rocky Gravino and Don Delano. As he stood beside the newspaper publisher, Don looked uncertain as to whether he wished to linger, his expression changing to relief when he spied Gracie.

"Good morning, gentlemen."

Rocky answered her. "Hi, Gracie. Out for your morning walk, eh?"

Don grinned. "Good morning, Gracie! How's your ham actor doing today?"

She laughed. "Thanks again. Had it been a real emergency . . . anyway, I'm grateful. What are we watching?"

The action seemed centered not on the police station but on the street in front of the building. Beyond the onlookers, a fire truck lolled at the curb, only a few of its many lights flashing. Firefighters walked about in T-shirts, huge boots, and baggy clown pants with yellow suspenders. But their big, heavy turnout coats lay in an orderly stack on the truck's running board, so they weren't fighting a fire.

A young woman firefighter with her blond hair pulled back came out of the station carrying a huge fan. Gracie heard her tell the chief, "That's about as much as we can do."

Rocky explained, "They're exhausting the building."

"That's amazing!" Gracie watched the police chief shake his head wearily. "It doesn't even look out of breath."

Rocky started to explain, "I mean, they're using huge fans to blow all the stink out.

Like —" but then he caught on that he'd been snookered. "You know what I mean. Like when they air out a fire-damaged building, clear the smoke away."

"Has anyone any idea what happened? What that smell was last night?"

Don, a chemistry teacher, had no doubts. "You can tell from a mile away. It was hydrogen sulfide. Rotten egg gas."

"That was the smell in the church, too. Rotten eggs! Years ago, El wanted something to clear his sinuses. So I started to make him a chili pepper omelet, one of his favorites."

Don whistled. "That would do it."

"I broke open the first egg," Gracie continued, "and a moment later, it not only had cleared El's sinuses, it also cleared the house and most of the block. It's a stink that really spreads and permeates, just as it did at the church."

Rocky arched one eyebrow. "This isn't a reflection on your cooking, is it?"

"No, but it's a reflection on Frank Billingsly's chickens. He used to save some fertile eggs for me, back when he was running that hatchery. He saved one of them a little too long." Gracie looked at Don. "What makes rotten egg gas? Besides eggs, I mean."

"Mischief makers. Kids. Just about anybody. It's not hard to make, if you know how. A few ingredients easily found around the home, and presto. You have a highly effective stink bomb."

"Or just let some eggs rot and throw 'em." Rocky did not look amused. "This is becoming more than a minor nuisance. Somebody is deliberately doing this. Has to be a reason why."

Gracie heard a familiar voice. Roy Bell, the contractor, stepped in beside them. "Warms the cockles of a fellow's heart, don't it?" He obviously was enjoying Chief Bowers' frustrated gestures and shoulder shrugs.

Gracie understood. "You got another ticket, didn't you, Roy?"

"None of your concern, Ms. Nosy," he snapped at her. "I don't need to hear from you."

Gracie's recent insight about Roy's short fuse came back to her. What had been true at the feed store was still the case.

Don strode by Gracie to stand in front of Roy. "Now, Roy. I've known Gracie Parks for years and years, even before I joined the Eternal Hope choir. And I know she's always had the welfare of everyone else at heart, and that includes yours. So I suggest you should be grateful that she cares about you and speak more respectfully to her, don't you think?"

Don's baritone voice carried so much weight that Roy moved back a step. Gracie, meanwhile, wouldn't have interpreted the look on his face as fear, exactly, but it showed a powerful concern.

Roy shifted subjects. "The cops are too high and mighty lately. That's all. This little accident, it serves 'em right. That's what I was saying."

Rocky broke in. "Hm. Gracie said 'another' ticket. In this state, if you get too many of those things, they can take away your license. I'm trying to imagine you bicycling to work with paint cans hanging from the handlebars. Having a hard time picturing it."

Roy snorted. "Gotta go. Somebody in this town has to work, and I don't see any of you doing it." He slipped out from between the two men and marched away.

Gracie said with mock meekness, "Uh, er, thank you both for coming to my defense. But, uh, perhaps —"

"I loved it!" Don exulted. "I hardly ever get the chance to lean on anyone. Thanks for the opportunity."

Gracie noted, "He *was* upset by the tickets. He's usually very polite."

"How many tickets?" Rocky asked. "And do you suppose he'd be upset enough to stink-bomb the police station?"

"So he has a grudge against the cops. But then, why," Don asked, "would he bomb the church? On a Wednesday evening, yet?"

He looked at Gracie. "How many tickets has he gotten, anyway?"

Gracie waved as she walked off. "That would be gossip, and I don't do gossip. Enjoy the beautiful day, gentlemen." She winked at them as she repositioned her earpieces.

The tape she was listening to featured instrumental versions of old favorite hymns, and she liked the B side even better than the A. She particularly appreciated the fact that they kept "Mighty Fortress" rolling at a good tempo. Under her breath, she sang along with the final rousing chorus. Then she picked up the pace with "I Saw the Light."

The early sunlight had turned from gold to white. It made the streets and houses sparkle. Gracie loved her little town with special intensity on mornings like this, when Willow Bend seemed to glow.

As she came around the corner a block

from home, she saw her uncle. He was standing in front of their house in his walker, quite obviously watching for her. The moment he spotted her, he began waving his arms, signalling, *Hurry! Hurry! Come!*

9

Gracie broke into a jog, moving even quicker than the tempo of the "Old Rugged Cross" in her ears.

Uncle Miltie had a fussbudget's tendency to worry about insignificant things. Now, however, he was upset enough to be standing in the street wearing his robe and house slippers.

"It's Gooseberry again!" he shouted as she approached. "And if he's faking death this time, he should get an Academy Award!" Uncle Miltie's walker clunked behind her into the house. "Not the mantel. He's under your bed. I couldn't reach him."

She hurried to her room. Under the bed meant something serious. Gooseberry went there only when he was very frightened or feeling very ill.

"Gooseberry?" Gracie stepped inside her bedroom. She fished her flashlight from the nightstand drawer and lay down beside the bed. "Gooseberry." She lifted the dust ruffle.

The flashlight beam swept back and forth. There he was, all curled up, scrunched as tightly against the wall as he could manage.

"Gooseberry? Come to me, Sweetie."

He did not move or look at her.

No response.

Behind her, Uncle Miltie asked, "Is he all right?"

"I don't think so." Gracie abandoned her flashlight and began torturously to wriggle herself under the bed. She had fit just fine in a space this size — when she was seven. Now, she ended up laboriously dragging the bed away from the wall.

She stretched for a grip on Gooseberry. His soft, familiar fur felt comforting in her hand as she scooped and pulled him toward her. She sat on the floor and leaned back against the side of her bed as she cradled the limp cat on her arm. Scratching under his chin, a favorite spot, did not arouse him.

Uncle Miltie braced in his walker. "He's not faking this time, is he." It was a statement, not a question. It required no answer. Uncle Miltie's concern was clearly expressed in his face.

Gracie clambered to her feet as Gooseberry lay limp in her awkward embrace. "I'll call you when I know something." She hurried downstairs with him and straight out to the garage. She laid the cat on the passenger seat, hit the garage door button, and jammed her key in the ignition.

No, that was the trunk key. She jammed the other key into the ignition.

Every now and then, Gooseberry used to cast a hairball or make a mess or appear to feel a bit under the weather. But never had he been ill like this. Never.

She backed distractedly out onto the street. Old Mrs. Martin, coming up the street in that thirty-year-old Cadillac of hers, had to swerve to avoid hitting her. Mrs. Martin blared her horn in passing. Gracie waved grimly.

It would take her nine minutes to reach her regular vet's, not counting the seven minutes it always took to pry Gooseberry out from under the sofa whenever he saw her get his travel box out. He did not particularly fancy vets. On the other hand, the All Creatures Small Animal Clinic, Davena Wilkins, DVM, was less than a three-minute drive. She went directly there.

As she burst into the clinic office, Gracie did not even have to say "Emergency!" The receptionist saw her come in, glanced at the limp cat, and hurried out from behind the counter. "This way!"

Gracie followed breathlessly.

Halfway down a modest hallway, the girl waved a hand. "In here. The doctor will be right there."

Gracie carried Gooseberry into a quiet little examination room. She was trembling. She had not noticed that until just now.

A young black woman in green scrubs came hurrying in. "What do we have?"

"I don't know. He's never done this before, Dr. Wilkins."

The vet was businesslike. Swiftly, expertly, she began the examination. She opened his mouth and sniffed. She buried her nose in his fur and sniffed. "Where has he been?"

"I don't know." Gracie moved in close and sniffed also. Why had she not noticed it right away? She had been too upset, apparently. "He had that same strange smell yesterday! And he seemed a little ill, but not anything like this. True, he's not exactly a young cat. . . ."

"Gooseberry. Why Gooseberry?" Dr. Wilkins lifted the cat and cradled him as if he were her own. Gracie liked that. The woman headed for the door. "Come with me, please."

"It made me laugh, I guess. And I do love

gooseberries." Gracie suddenly remembered that wonderful moment of deciding on a name for her already spoiled orange kitten. Her eyes teared.

The veterinarian led the way to the far end of the hall. "This is our quiet room." She pushed the door open and kept her voice very low. "As I'm sure you know, cats like to hide when they don't feel well. So we give them a hidey hole. You can come in at any time to visit Gooseberry, but we do want to keep him here. You probably noticed his pupils are dilated. I suspect poisoning of some sort. We'll run tests, of course, and let you know what we find."

Gently, she slipped him into a low, dark box, a cubbyhole much like a space far beneath a bed. Reluctant to leave, Gracie reached in and stroked the proud old fur. The cat did not respond. The tears spilled onto Gracie's cheeks.

This certainly was a quiet room. But the silence was rudely broken when the receptionist came rushing in, obviously agitated; still, she kept her voice to a hoarse whisper. "Mrs. Lawrence just brought in her Shih Tzu, Charlotte. It looks bad."

10

One of the traits Gracie shared with the family she'd married into was a healthy sense of curiosity. She remembered fondly her father-in-law, Henry Parks, joking, "How can something be healthy when it gets you into trouble so often?" But curiosity, of course, could be useful, too.

Gracie's need to know seized her now. She really should continue straight back out to the waiting room like a good patient. Instead, she followed Dr. Wilkins to the next examination. She had to see; she had to know.

At the doorway, she exclaimed, "Oh, no, Marge! Not Charlotte too!" even as Marge was exclaiming, "Oh, no, Gracie! Not Gooseberry too!"

Dr. Wilkins looked from face to face. "Neighbors, I take it."

Gracie nodded. "Next door. But the animals keep a respectful distance."

"That's not true!" Marge insisted. "Your

Gooseberry thinks he's a dog."

"Well, I'll admit he has a few little doglike habits."

"A few?!" Marge sniffed.

"So he follows me around and likes to dig. And fetch things. Charlotte's a little catlike herself."

Marge ignored this and turned to Dr. Wilkins. "Charlotte somehow squeezed under the fence while I was at work yesterday." Forlornly, she watched the doctor examine the little Shih Tzu. "I don't let her run. This time she escaped and I didn't know it."

"Could the two have gone somewhere together?" The vet sniffed closely at the dog's mouth and fur.

Gracie shrugged. "It's not impossible. But mostly they act like only children." On impulse she stepped in close and sniffed as well. She detected that same vague smell. "They *watch* each other."

"Charlotte wouldn't go very far," Marge protested. "I'm not saying she's lazy, exactly, but she doesn't like to go out of her way too much."

"This business is getting worrisome." The vet scooped Charlotte up in her arms. "I need to keep her overnight so we can run some tests."

"Of course!" Marge stepped aside.

Dr. Wilkins carried Charlotte out the door, so Gracie followed. But they turned down a little side passageway.

"Not the quiet room?" Gracie asked.

"Dogs bark."

One could not argue with that statement. With Marge and Gracie at her heels, the vet placed Charlotte in a dog box in a room at the end of the hall.

Charlotte did not seem as sick as Gooseberry; she still responded, and gave Marge's hand a lick when Marge delivered a goodbye pat. But her tail wasn't wagging.

The two friends thanked the doctor, filled out forms at the front desk, and walked out the door from gloom into sunshine.

Marge pointed to her car. "Get in. Bagel time."

They rode downtown together in Marge's car to their friend Abe Wasserman's deli. There Abe himself, proprietor and chief cook, was behind his counter as usual.

"Gracie, Marge — the best of all that God gives, my dears. What will you have?"

Marge leaned forward to survey the array of baked goods under the glass. As she did so, Gracie whispered to Abe, "We've just come from the vet's. Both Gooseberry and Charlotte are ill, and we don't have any idea why. It's horrible!" She put her finger to her lips. "Sshh, I'm going to try to keep Marge distracted for a few minutes here. Some of your wonderful sweet rolls will help."

He nodded, looking somber.

Marge chose a cinnamon twist and Gracie a plain bagel with cream cheese. Taking their plates and cups of milky coffee, they went to sit at the little table in the window. As they began to eat, Abe continued to watch over them, as he bustled about his morning clean-up.

The door opened and Harry Durant came ambling in. He seemed never to move faster than a slow walk. His shop coveralls, as usual, were all oil- and grease-spotted. Gracie knew his wife kept a fastidious house, but it would always be hard to tell from Harry's appearance.

"Your usual?" Abe asked the new customer, reaching for the doughnut tray.

"Yep, but double it. Just got done talking with my lawyer. It'd make any man weep." He made a face, and addressed Gracie and Marge, too. "Did you know we can't get an injunction against that company that's coming in? That factory? I might get me a new lawyer, someone willing to take them on." He licked a bit of sugar off his finger.

"Take on whom?"

Impatiently, Harry told them, "The factory that's coming in, that's who! They been scouting the area now for a week. In cahoots with that preacher. I'm all ready to file an injunction, but the namby-pamby lawyer says you can't." Now he had sugar on his chin.

"Why not? Enlighten me." Abe poured a cup of coffee.

Gracie smiled to herself at Abe's subtle invitation to talk. She herself had succumbed to it many a time.

Harry took a bite of doughnut and explained with his mouth full. "He says, before we can do anything, they have to make an offer or announce a location. Then we can protest it. You know what that means. It means we wait until after the cat's out of the bag, and then we get to try to catch it and stuff it back in. I say, just throw the whole bag in the river right away."

Gracie closed her eyes.

Gooseberry.

11

The house was so quiet. It sounded quiet. It felt quiet. The silence reverberated on Gracie's heart. Gooseberry was not a noisy cat by any means. His presence had never added significantly to the house's voice, its many odd little sounds. Why did his absence make the house echo now, hollow?

Gracie adjusted herself in her favorite chair by the front room window. When the doorbell rang she realized she had actually dozed off over her book. For a moment, at least, she'd stopped worrying. Now, holding her place because she had forgotten to pick up a bookmark before she sat down, she answered the door.

Jessica Larson, beaming proudly, swooped in, her fourteen-year-old genius at her heels. Jeffrey Larson, boy chemist, did look a little odd without his eyebrows. He wore the uniform of the junior high student — the cap, baggy pants and T-shirt that every single other fourteen-year-old boy wore in order to look different.

"Please come in. Have a seat." She led the way into the front room. Behind her, she heard Uncle Miltie descending the stairs.

Jessica perched demurely on the sofa. Jeffrey sprawled in El's old easy chair.

Uncle Miltie completed his descent.

Jessica pointed to the book in Gracie's hand. "What are you reading?"

"*Apothecary Rose*. It's a mystery set in medieval York, in England. Candace Robb. She is brilliant at putting you into the era and the scene."

"Oh. I don't like English mysteries. Except Agatha Christie, of course." She smiled sweetly. "Jeffrey, dear, explain why we're here."

Jeffrey started to open his mouth. Then he spied Uncle Miltie entering the front room, and he froze.

Uncle Miltie leaned into his walker. "Well, well, well. Hello, Jeffrey."

Jeffrey mumbled a greeting.

"Jeffrey?" Jessica's voice turned sharp.

Uncle Miltie grinned wickedly. "The cat got your tongue, boy?" Now why did he emphasize *cat* so weirdly, as if there were a conspiracy of some sort between the two of them?

With a brief, disapproving scowl at her

son, Jessica turned to Gracie and smiled sweetly. "I don't know if you heard. Jeffrey has been chosen to attend a science camp this summer. A very exclusive camp. Only the best applicants are allowed to attend."

Gracie nodded. "My congratulations, Jeffrey."

But Jeffrey apparently didn't hear her. His whole attention seemed riveted on Uncle Miltie. And yet, he was assiduously avoiding the old man's gaze.

Uncle Miltie kadumped across the room and sat in his favorite chair.

Jessica rolled on. "They have the very latest of everything — computers, laboratory equipment. The biology campers can even dissect things. Naturally, a camp like that is very expensive."

"Naturally." Gracie had a bad feeling about the direction this conversation was taking. She began planning her response, just in case her hunch was right.

"You see, just now, Ed's business has slowed down a bit. And so he agreed, reluctantly, I admit, that it might be all right if we approached a few close friends. You know, to help out a little."

Gracie, who had never felt close to Jessica, hated this sort of thing, mostly because what she dearly wanted to tell her visitor was so at odds with what she would actually say. "Jessica, I think it's wonderful that Jeffrey is so talented but, ah, we have to budget quite closely."

Jessica's smile never for a moment left her face, but its whole nature changed. "You did a wonderful job with Jeffrey's birthday party." The voice hardened to match the smile. "I'm sure you want those special catering jobs to keep coming from me and my friends."

Gracie didn't allow herself to rise to the bait. "I'm sorry, Jessica, but we can't help out. I do recognize that it was difficult to come and ask."

The false semblance of geniality fled. "I see." Jessica snapped to her feet. "Thank you for your time, Gracie. Jeffrey?"

But her son was already headed for the door. Gracie wondered if the boy would be polite enough to hold the door open for his mother as she left.

He wasn't. In fact, he hustled out ahead of her.

From the doorway, Gracie called goodbye as the two marched down the sidewalk. She thought, to her surprise, she heard Jeffrey saying to his mother, "Why didn't you warn me? I didn't know this was where that old guy lived."

She closed the door and returned to the front room. "Okay, what's going on between you and Jeffrey?"

"You handled that extortion attempt real well, Gracie. Better'n I would've. If I were twenty years younger and a thousand percent spryer, I would've wrapped my walker around her ears."

"If you were younger and spryer you wouldn't have the walker. What about Jeffrey?"

"I was walking down by Fairweather Park early one morning last week. I saw this kid with a burlap bag, and the bag was moving. Something alive in it. His back was turned to me. He pulls this big black cat out of the bag, all trussed up. Then he pulls a bottle of something out of his pocket. When I got close enough to see what was happening, he was trying to force the cat to drink something in a bottle."

"Getting a cat to drink if it doesn't want to. . . ."

"And it wasn't, either. I yelled at him. He dropped the cat and ran. I used to know the Larson kid when I saw him, but this time I didn't recognize him — he's older and bigger and has that new haircut. Took me ten minutes to get the cat untied. It was wrapped in masking tape."

Gracie thought a moment. "A big black cat. A tom?"

"Didn't notice. Wasn't getting much co-operation from it." He frowned. "Why?"

"Do you remember? I'm sure I mentioned it. A week ago, Mrs. Benton's cat was one of the first to fall sick with this mysterious whatever-it-is. Her cat is a big black tom."

12

Of all the things Gracie Lynn Parks firmly believed in, giving back to God the best of everything was one of the firmest. To that end, she had purchased not the cheapest potatoes for the church's potato salad, or even the fancy baking russets, but the elegant, buttery, Yukon Golds. For flavor and texture, nothing can match a Yukon Gold.

She lifted the lid on her cast iron pot, paused while the gush of steam lifted away, and gently prodded a potato with her fork. Five more minutes. She set to chopping the rest of the celery.

The doorbell rang. From the front of the house came Uncle Miltie's, "I'll get it."

Moments later, Rocky Gravino's bulk filled the kitchen doorway. "Hello, Gracie. Smells good."

He always said that, whether anything aromatic were cooking or not. Gracie strongly suspected it was a sly and subtle hint that he wouldn't turn down something to eat.

"Good afternoon, Rocky. I'm glad you stopped by. Since I was boiling eggs for the potato salad anyway, I cooked up some extras to try out a *new* deviled egg recipe. Tell me what you think." She fetched the plastic egg tray out of the refrigerator and popped the lid. "Coffee?"

"Sure, if it's made."

"I was thinking of brewing myself some. Five minutes." She set about grinding coffee beans.

He peered appreciatively at the array of eggs. "I heard your cat was sick and so is the next-door neighbor's dog."

"That's right. The veterinarian doesn't know what it is. She's running tests."

"She. That'd be Dave Wilkins, right? She's good. If anyone can figure it out, she can." Cautiously, he chose one garnished with paprika and a few leaves of parsley.

Gracie made note that this particular combination of green with reddish seemed to have good eye appeal. "She impressed me quite favorably."

He bit, paused, and savored, staring again at the Las Vegas souvenir dice by the refrigerator. "Did you put mayo in this?"

"Very little. Just a tiny dollop in the whole batch, for moisture." She poured water in the coffeemaker well.

85

"Good. I'm not a big mayo fan. This is excellent. So if the dog got sick too, it's not feline distemper or something like that."

"I suspect the vet would recognize that quickly."

He nodded. "You know, people are getting sick, too. Five in the last twenty-four hours ended up in the emergency room. Looks like food poisoning but not quite. Know what I mean? And then there were those sheep, and Pete Murphy's dog. Think something really virulent is starting the rounds? An epidemic if we don't watch out?" This time he chose one of the ones made darker with a bit of Worcestershire.

Gracie sat down across from him. "I should think a veterinarian would know better than I. Or the public health department. Did you talk to anyone like that?"

"Yeah, I just got done interviewing the large-animal man Frank Billingsly uses. But hey." Rocky heaved his shoulders in a what-can-you-do? shrug. "You know vets. They make their money off sick animals, whether their patients live or die. Would they be real quick to jump on it? The guy could be lying."

Gracie felt her mouth drop open. "Rocco Gravino, I'm appalled! What a cynical attitude!"

"Call it the skeptic in me. All newspaper people are skeptics." But apparently he could sense when to let go of a subject. "These are really good. Say, Gracie! You know, that new factory is going to hire hundreds of people. They're going to have a full employee cafeteria. Know what you might do, if you wanted a real job? Apply for a position as their kitchen manager. They're going to need a good cook."

"How do you know all this?" She went back to the kitchen counter. Watched coffeemakers never boil.

"If you're looking for a site, where's the first place you go?"

"A realtor?"

"The local newspaper." He plucked another half-egg. "Realtors try to sell you what they're listing. The newspaper knows the lowdown. Whom to call, where the good stuff is, what are the places to avoid. And we're county-wide. Smart, to call on the newspaper editor first."

"So you've been talking to the plant's scout." She got two mugs from the cupboard. On second thought . . . she brought a third down also. As soon as the aroma reached Uncle Miltie, he'd be here.

"Gracie, this company's gonna do big things for the area."

"You sound like this factory thing is a done deal."

"It is. If they can't get Frank's sheep pasture, they have some alternative sites in mind. Whatever, it's gonna go. But they want Frank's place the most."

"Our pastor is in favor of it. To boost employment."

Rocky nodded. "One of the very few things we agree on, Meyer and me."

Gracie smiled as she brought the pot to the table. "You say a few things. What's another?" Well she did know his avoidance of most things religious.

"We can usually agree on the color of the grass. Not always."

Uncle Miltie clumped through the kitchen doorway. "I smell coffee."

The phone rang. It always waited until she had a coffeepot in her hand. She picked up the receiver and went back to the table to pour. "Hello."

"Mrs. Parks? This is Dr. Wilkins."

"How is Gooseberry?"

"Still alive, but that's about all. I've run all the standard tests. Nothing. And I called your regular vet to pick his brain, since he knows your cat best. I was hoping he might have some insight. Unfortunately, he's stymied, too. In fact, he just lost a cat. Same symptoms." She paused. "Mrs. Parks?"

"I'm listening. I don't know what to say, except that I'm grateful for all your efforts."

"We'll put our heads together and do our best. But I can't say it looks good. We can all pray, too." She hung up, promising to phone again at the end of the day.

Gracie, meanwhile, was already starting to follow her advice.

13

Gracie stood on her front porch watching Rocky leave. She waved as he pulled away from the curb. As she started back inside, she suddenly stopped. It was a beautiful day, pleasant to bask in. Why was she in such a hurry to go inside? She closed the door behind her and sat down in her porch rocker.

Gooseberry's furry image crowded itself into her head and filled it, snuffing out rational thought. Like all cats, the inscrutable Gooseberry exercised his own secret criteria for accepting or rejecting people, and he had accepted Gracie unconditionally. Although he was civil and decent toward Uncle Miltie, he did not accept the man in the same unreserved way. Gooseberry. So thoroughly cat; so uniquely himself. Gracie knew that, at some time, she was bound to lose him. Human beings outlive cats, and that's that. But not this way. Not this way.

She took her concerns right to the top.

*God, thank You for the perfect animal com-
panion. I put him in Your hands, and I sure
would appreciate some more time with him.*

How long had she been sitting here? She
had no idea. But she still felt quite weary.
She got up and went inside.

In the front room, Uncle Miltie was nodding off in his favorite chair, snoring gently.
His head drooped at what looked like a most
uncomfortable angle. Should she wake him?
She decided against it.

In fact, it wasn't such a bad idea. Perhaps
she herself should take a brief nap before
facing the youth group this evening. The
notion appealed mightily. She wanted to
shake this sadness, this lethargy.

She paused at the foot of the stairs. What
was that noise? It was dripping of an odd
sort. The dishwasher had finished its run, so
it couldn't be that. She veered away from
the stairs and headed for the kitchen.

Water greeted her at the kitchen door.
Nearly an inch of it . . . on the floor where
water ought never to be . . . soaking into the
dining room carpet . . . all over. . . .

Panic welled up and numbed her brain.

She waded out across her poor kitchen
floor, sploshing. When she slipped and
nearly fell, she realized she must be more
careful. She shoved open the back door. A

91

miniature Niagara poured out the door and down the stoop.

She blocked the door open and didn't even bother trying to seek the source. She ran to the shed and grabbed the T-wrench, ran out front to the water valve, and yanked the brass cover off. It took all her strength to get the valve closed, cutting off the whole system. When it was as tight as she could make it, she returned to the back door and stepped gingerly into her poor, sodden kitchen. The gurgling sound had ceased.

It took her five minutes and three different numbers before she managed to reach Roy Bell on his cell phone.

"I can be there in an hour or so," he promised.

With her wide broom and a heavy sigh — more than one sigh, actually — she began the laborious process of chasing water out the back door. It took her nearly an hour. She switched to the sponge mop eventually, but the floor was still wet when Roy got there.

He arrived an hour and a half after her call. For him, that was prompt. He stepped into her kitchen and looked warily about.

Gracie sighed yet again. She remembered

her last meeting with him. "The cat's not here. You're safe."

"Good."

"You really dislike cats, Roy."

"Hate 'em. Always have. Dogs, too. Digging under your fence and chasing the chickens, cats using your flowerbeds for a sandbox and ripping out the flowers, know what I mean? Pests, all of 'em." With that curmudgeonly commentary, he pulled his flashlight out of his pocket and set off to find the source.

He opened the double cabinet doors under the sink first, got on his knees and peered inside. "Remember when I said you should get these pipes replaced?"

"I remember." Gracie knelt beside him.

"Well, I meant it." He shone his light on a pipe at the back. "Ran your dishwasher, right?"

"Yes."

"Overloaded the system once too often. See the rupture?"

Yes. She could see the blown-out pipe, now that he pointed it out. "How much is involved in fixing it? How long will it take?"

"I'll see what I have on my truck. I think I got what I need to fix it now. Half an hour for a temporary repair. But you better just get this whole kitchen replumbed. Old houses like this, their plumbing don't last forever."

"Fix it temporarily, if you can. I'll start another pot of coffee when the water's back on. Cobbler?"

"Wouldn't dream of turning you down." He pocketed his flashlight as he went out the back door.

He toted in two heavy toolboxes. The standard joke around town, not altogether funny but altogether true, was that Roy Bell charged by the toolbox. Gracie winced, therefore, when he went back out and returned with two more toolboxes. These were filled not with tools but with odd pipe fittings of various substances and colors.

The man might not like small animals (a mark against him in any cat person's book), but he was a whiz at fixing things (a huge mark on the plus side for anyone with a plumbing problem like Gracie's). In less than half an hour he sat at Gracie's table, the water turned back on and his toolboxes closed up and sitting by the door, munching cherry cobbler.

"Tell me something. Jessica Larson didn't happen to tap you for a donation to send her kid to camp, did she?"

Gracie frowned. "She asked you too?"

"Aha. She hinted that if I wanted to fix her

windows any more, I better pony up. She made me mad."

Gracie smiled. "I take it you turned her down, right?"

"Told her I didn't need her windows." He forked in another mouthful of cobbler. "I get the feeling she's not used to people talking to her like that."

Gracie nodded. "Some people court trouble. You don't have to. You just open the door and it walks right in."

"Okay, look at me," Roy said. "You needed help fast and I came fast. Now that kind of service just don't happen in your big cities. You can wait for days for a plumber and then you don't know what kind of quality you're getting. Me, I provide top quality."

"Oh, I agree."

He wagged his finger. "Speed and quality command top price, and you pay it. In fact, I charge you a little less because you don't try to squeeze me. You recognize my value, know what I mean?"

"I'm grateful."

"Now Jessica, she's always trying to get me to do the job for less. Haggles over every dime. So if she never asks me to do something for her again, it won't hurt me none at all. Got enough good customers that I don't need the likes of her."

Gracie glanced at the clock. She was going to have to take her potato salad to the church before long.

With the side of his fork, Roy scraped up the last bits of filling. "Did you sign the petition yet?"

"What petition?"

"Harry Durant and I, we're circulating a petition. You know Frank Billingsly's pasture where that factory's planning on building."

Down inside, Gracie moaned *not the factory again,* but she kept it to herself. "What about it?"

"Part of it's wetland. We think the state ought to block the deal because of ruining the wetland. There's laws against that, you know what I mean? You gotta protect wetland."

"I have my own wetland, homegrown. Do you suppose the law includes kitchen floors and dining room carpet?"

Roy chuckled. "Here." He got up and went over to one of his many toolboxes. He rummaged through the largest of them and returned to the table with a cylindrical box. "This stuff prevents mildew. Sprinkle it good on your wet carpet."

"Thank you! How much do I owe you?"

He waved a hand. "That cobbler makes us even. It was delicious. Gotta get going. Call me when you need me."

Gracie led him to the door and helped him carry his toolboxes out to his truck. When she returned to the house she glanced in at Uncle Miltie in his easy chair.

He was still snoring. She left him a note next to the cobbler where he'd be sure to find it.

14

Every grandmother who keeps the grandkids for any longer than, say, five minutes, learns what Gracie Parks had long known: even the best little kids just plain wear you out. Gracie loved being around children of all ages. She got along well with them. She enjoyed their exuberance and idealism, and their quixotic sense of fairness. But they always left her exhausted.

Tonight, the choir was hosting a hot dog roast for the youth group in the church basement. The youth group, electric in its enthusiasm, drained Gracie's energy by osmosis every time she worked with them or even near them.

Gracie arrived early at the church, her slaw recipe in hand and a big bowl of her Yukon Gold potato salad on the car seat beside her. She stashed her purse in her choir locker and headed to the kitchen to work.

Lester called, "Here she is! Gracie, do you put onions in the beans now or later?"

"How thin do we shave the cabbage?" Don Delano turned toward her, pointing to the cutting board beside him.

Amy Cantrell was just tying on an apron. "Gracie, how many tablespoons of relish are in a jar?"

Gracie looked at each one in turn. She said to Lester, "Now," to Don, "Very," and to Amy, "That depends. What size jar and has it been opened?" She set her potato salad on the work table and retrieved her own apron from the hook by the tin pie safe.

Don grabbed a teaspoon and crossed to the potato salad. "Quality control," he announced. "We can't be too careful."

Estelle Livett glared at him. "Touch that and I break your hand."

Don laid the spoon down. "I'll just take this out to the buffet table." He scooped up the bowl and left.

Under normal circumstances, Gracie loved a job like this. In fact, preparing for the youth group's annual hot dog feast was one of her favorites. Her experienced help and culinary contributions were appreciated by the rest of the kitchen volunteers as well as the kids, and that certainly added to the pleasure. But best of all, she was serving God in God's house by doing something she truly enjoyed. It couldn't get much better than that.

Except tonight. Thoughts of her poor Gooseberry, still alive but laid so low, weighed upon her heavily. She was supposed to orchestrate the creation of her renowned slaw, but found she could not concentrate. Her stern admonitions to herself usually did their job. This time, *Now you shape up, Gracie Lynn Parks!* didn't work.

Marge arrived, the winds of haste tossing her carefully shaped curls all askew. "Sorry I'm late. I was at the vet's." She looked at Gracie. "I looked in on Gooseberry too." She didn't need to explain that there was no good news.

Don Delano looked up from slicing the cabbage. "There has to be some kind of clear answer to this. What would kill sheep and make other animals ill?"

"People too, perhaps," Lester added.

"People too. And since animals have died, there is the strong possibility people might as well. This isn't something to sit on our hands and wonder about. Apparently no one else is working on a solution. We should be."

Rick Harding came through the door. "Solution to what?"

Don put his knife down. "The agent attacking animals and maybe people. Rick, you're a computer expert. Can you research the symptoms and see what's out there?"

Rick stood in thought a moment. "I'm no biochemist. I'm a computer nerd. But I'll see what I can do."

Computer nerd? Gracie had to say such a description didn't perfectly describe this large black man with the sweet grin and lovely tenor voice. She smiled at him.

Amy offered, "A friend of mine is an herbalist. In fact, she's coming to the supper tonight. We can get her to show us her books and see what we find."

Don looked interested. "Good! And I'll try to get my hands on the toxicology reports, if there are any, and trace down sources for any chemicals they suggest."

Barb Jennings paused in the kitchen doorway. "Let's get moving, folks. The kids are starting to arrive."

Gracie picked up the condiments tray and went out into the dining hall. Over by the stairwell door, Roy Bell was talking to Harry Durant. The two Bell children and Harry's grandson were already running around yelling.

She stopped beside the potato salad because Jeffrey Larson was hovering over it altogether too eagerly.

His friend Roger saw Gracie and sucked in air. He stood transfixed, wide-eyed.

She put the condiments down and raised a finger in stern warning. "No nibbling until the pastor says grace."

Jeffrey glanced resentfully toward her and walked away. With a shake of her head, she returned to the kitchen.

Don was just finishing the last of the cabbage. Lester loaded a serving cart with dishes and flatware. Gracie stirred the slaw dressing, then sniffed to determine how much more rice vinegar it needed.

Marge paused by Gracie's elbow and frowned at the big steel bowl. She swiped her rubber spatula along the bowl rim and tasted. "I thought you usually put sugar in this recipe."

"Of course I . . . oh no!" She hadn't! Gracie hurried to the cupboard. It was the wrong time to add sugar, but the recipe was a simple one and really quite forgiving. It was not lost. It would still work. She grabbed the bag of sugar. "What could I be thinking of?!"

"Your cat," Marge replied. "Here. You add and I'll stir."

The two friends went through seven spoons tasting and adding and tasting again, getting the sweet-sour flavor of sugar and rice vinegar balanced just right. As one, they nodded to each other. Don helped them toss the dressing with the cabbage and diced carrots, then carried the big steel bowl out into the dining area.

Estelle handed Lester a mammoth basket of hot dog buns; they were all aware that a *lot* of hot dog buns are necessary to feed a hungry youth group.

Pastor Paul was bringing in a batch of gas-grilled wieners. From the warming oven, Marge retrieved the first ones he had already cooked. Paul then headed back out into the dining room with a big, flat pan of hot dogs. It takes a lot of wieners to feed a youth group, too.

Gracie paused to listen as he said grace and invited the kids to table. As a member of the youth group as well as of the choir, Amy went out into the dining room to join her friends.

As she commenced the next chore — cleaning up — Gracie offered still another prayer for Gooseberry. She felt just a wee bit foolish making prayers for a cat when so many human beings all over the world were suffering. On the other hand, when God told her to cast all her cares upon Him, she assumed He meant it. Significant in the scheme of world humanitarian concerns or not, Gooseberry was a great care to her just now.

While she was at it, she thanked God for sending Marge by at the right time to catch her recipe error. Without sugar, what a disaster that would have been! She could just envision their uninhibited young guests announcing, "This stuff tastes funny!"

"This stuff tastes funny!" Here came Amy back into the kitchen. She thrust her plate toward Gracie. "The potato salad tastes like bananas."

"Oh come!" Gracie grabbed a spoon and dipped a bit from Amy's plate.

The potato salad tasted like a banana.

"It's impossible." Gracie stared at the serving. "My potato salad has never been close to a banana. Not even the same room!" She tried to think. Actually, that was not true. Uncle Miltie, instructed by one of his doctors to eat a banana a day, kept a bunch in the hanging wire basket by the sink.

"I like pineapple on pizza, but this isn't the same thing." Amy looked forlornly at her plate.

"I'm sorry," was the only response Gracie could think of.

Amy wandered back out to the dining area. Within five minutes, seven other people, Lester Twomley among them, came back to the kitchen to ask Gracie why she had put bananas in the potato salad.

Could Uncle Miltie, who liked bad jokes, have played a practical one? Somehow, when she wasn't watching, could he have sliced up one or more of his bananas in her salad? That had to be it. Bananas are about the same shade of off-white as cooked potatoes, in fact. But when? The potatoes had not been out of her sight. She tried mentally to retrace everything she'd done all day. She could not.

And would Uncle Miltie do something silly and wasteful like this? She doubted it.

There was no way she could have made a mistake like that, was there? Her lunch had included a banana. Could she have sliced a banana, inadvertently put it in with the potatoes and. . . .

Oh surely not! Even worrying about Gooseberry, she wasn't that addled.

The rest of the evening dissolved in a muddle. She was so tired. And it wasn't just the youth group's enthusiasm that did it, either. But, as she went about cleaning up the kitchen, Gracie did think of one practical thing that she could do.

She would retrace Gooseberry's steps on

the day he took ill, as best she could. It wouldn't hurt and, if luck descended, what she found might offer some clue. Having at last found something positive to do buoyed her spirits.

15

"That has got to be the craziest, most far-fetched nonsense I ever heard!" exclaimed her skeptical newspaperman friend. "And remember, I've covered presidential races. I'm an expert on the subject."

"Now what is so far-fetched about backtracking Gooseberry? Have some more coffee." Gracie emptied the pot into Rocky's mug before he could answer and sat down at her kitchen table across from him.

"Gracie, you're asking people to remember if an orange cat walked by! It's like asking someone how many telephone poles they just drove past. Nobody notices that kind of thing. It's a cat, for pete's sake!"

"I'll start at the back door and go east up the alley first."

"And besides, it's been two days." Rocky sipped coffee. "Who's going to remember seeing a cat two days ago?"

Gracie looked serene. "Rocky, you don't

have to come along if you think it's going to be so fruitless."

"What? A chance to tell you I told you so? I don't get many of those. I wouldn't miss it for the world." He folded his napkin beside his plate. "Lunch was excellent. Loved the little sandwiches. And to think I never even heard of salmon-flavored cream cheese."

"I suppose I should admit that I was using you as a guinea pig again. I'm thinking of adding them to my catering menu. I'm glad you liked them." For a moment, she watched him sip coffee.

Uncle Miltie came into the kitchen. The net bag slung across the front of his walker clinked with china sounds.

"Hello, Uncle Miltie," Rocky said. "Didn't realize you were home."

"Mmph." Uncle Miltie muttered something else as he clumped to the dishwasher. He commenced loading his empty dishes from the bag into the machine.

Rocky raised his eyebrows. "What's wrong?"

"That woman." When Uncle Miltie referred to Gracie as "that woman," he was angry indeed.

Gracie explained. "I accused him of putting chopped bananas in the potato salad, and he thinks I shouldn't have."

"Mmph!" Uncle Miltie uttered again and stomped out.

Gracie listened to his walker thump away down the hall. "It was the potato salad for our youth group function, a huge bowl of it. He says just maybe I could legitimately accuse him of sabotaging potato salad here at home — you know, a little batch — but not a huge batch at a public church event like that. He says his judgment isn't that poor and that I'm wrong to think it is."

Marge appeared at the back door, waved through its window, and came in.

Rocky turned in his chair. "H'lo, Marge."

She proceeded directly to the coffee pot, peered into it forlornly, and put it back. She frowned at Rocky. "So. What's up?"

"Heard on my police scanner that a S.W.A.T. team's on its way here. Figured I might as well warn Gracie, so she and her criminally inclined uncle can go on the lam before the coppers show up."

"You watch too many Edward G. Robinson movies."

"The best kind. Why are you here?"

"Gracie and I are going to find out where Charlotte and Gooseberry went, and where they would come across poison." She looked at Gracie accusingly. "Did you invite him along too?"

"Only after he arrived. He just happened to drop by."

"Oh. Of course." Marge dropped into the third chair. "I notice it's usually at meal times."

Rocky drained his mug on the way to the sink. He gave it a quick rinse and tucked it away in the dishwasher. "Guess we might as well get going. The quicker you ladies learn about the futility of chasing non-domesticated waterfowl, the better."

Gracie paused only long enough to call down the hallway, "We're leaving now, Uncle Miltie." The three would-be investigators trooped out the back door into sunshine as bright as Gracie's hopes. If only they would stumble across some clue! If only Gracie would be perceptive enough to recognize it when she saw it!

Gracie led the way across the backyard to the alley. "Cats have a habit of entry," she explained to Rocky. "That means, they enter and leave their territory by a certain pathway and try never to vary from that route. Gooseberry goes up this alley to the corner of Claybourne when he leaves, and he comes home along this alley."

"Then we ask Mrs. Finkmeyer first,"

Marge suggested. "She sees everything that goes on at that corner."

Rocky rolled his eyes. Gracie wondered if her decision to let him come along had been wise. Perhaps, when he showed up on her doorstep after she'd returned from church, she should have simply dismissed him. But then, she really had needed an objective take on those salmon-flavored sandwiches.

She thought about Gooseberry and couldn't help imagining wiping some of the salmon-flavored cream cheese off her sandwich spreader onto her finger and offering it to him. She could just feel his abrasive pink tongue, licking her finger cautiously at first, as if after all these years she might still try to give him something spinach-flavored.

The picture almost brought tears again to her eyes and she offered up a quick prayer.

Marge led the way across Claybourne to Mrs. Finkmeyer's little bungalow and stepped up on the porch. Rocky and Gracie moved in beside her. They stood there.

Rocky eventually asked, "Aren't you going to knock?"

Marge shook her head. "Don't have to. She knows we're here. It just takes her a bit to get from her rocking chair by the window to the door."

The door creaked. A woman the size of a

bud vase was peering out and then pushing her storm door open. "Come on in, Marge, Gracie."

They stepped inside. Gradually, Gracie's eyes adjusted to the gloom. Dark woodwork, dark floors and age-darkened wallpaper did nothing for the ambience.

Marge and Rocky were explaining their mission to Mrs. Finkmeyer. Gracie didn't hear it well because she was playing her usual game: Every time she entered Hallie Finkmeyer's house, she tried to spot something, anything, that had changed since her previous visit. Yet she had never once noticed anything different, not ever. On the other hand, each room was so cluttered with 1940s-era furniture and knickknacks, who could tell?

Mrs. Finkmeyer patted Gracie's arm. "I'm so glad you stopped by to ask. I've been thinking about you. I want to know how your cat is doing. I heard he's quite ill. I'm so sorry. I was just saying, I watched him go by two days ago, out on one of his little forays."

"I still can't believe it," Rocky objected. "You really remember seeing the cat?"

"Of course. He was headed home along on his usual route about seven forty-five in the morning. And that little dog of yours, Marge, was about half a block behind him."

16

Fairweather Park, or more officially Julius Norton Fairweather Memorial Park, offered something for everyone. Out by the street, a concrete ramps-and-loops area attracted daring skateboarders rendered immortal by reason of their youth. Huge grassy areas bordered by trees provided play space for soccer stars and football scrimmagers. Winding all through the extensive acreage of woodland and ponds, paved paths allowed access for strollers, in-line skaters and the wheelchair-bound.

And the benches: Most parks have park benches. The benches in Fairweather, though, all faced beauty of one sort or another, every one of them.

Gracie perched on the end of one of them looking out over the duck pond. She enjoyed watching the dozen fat birds waddle about. Now and then, a dark, glossy turtle would haul out to sun itself on a log anchored in the pond just for that purpose.

Marge sat at the other end. In the middle, Rocky was thoughtfully turning his ice cream cone, seeking to lick up the melting edges before they actually dripped.

"I don't know where to try next." Marge voiced Gracie's own thoughts aloud. "I suppose we could go down to that fruit stand on Route 18 and ask there."

"I'm amazed that you two have gotten this far," Rocky said.

"Ida Sharecroft had the best idea, I think." Gracie attended briefly to her own ice cream. "Ask at the school."

"Why?" Rocky shook his head. "If anyone's there that early, they'd be too busy to notice your peripatetic pets."

"Not the custodian," Marge replied. "He's a nosy old codger. He was there even when my boys were in school, and he was the same then, too. I just wish we could have gotten Hallie off the subject of that dratted factory long enough to learn something useful."

"What is it with these people?" Rocky fumed. "All I hear in this town is how rotten that factory is, and it isn't even a twinkle in anyone's eye yet. So it makes and sells auto parts. That's not so bad. Everybody needs them. Are people frightened of windshield wipers?"

Gracie suggested, "It's the change they're afraid of, my friend. Not the windshield wipers. And, I admit, some are more afraid than others."

"Afraid?" Rocky snorted. "Paranoid's more like it."

"Oh, look!" Gracie pointed to a thatch of green bobbing along toward the skateboard area. "Charles? Charles!"

The green-haired figure continued on its way.

"Chuckie Moon!" Gracie yelled, waving at him so he could see her.

Grudgingly, Chuckie now paused to look their way, glancing nervously toward the boys practicing wheelies beyond him. Obviously, it was way uncool to be seen interacting with a senior citizen.

Rocky took charge. "Hey, Moon. Get over here for a minute."

After a long moment of hesitation, Chuckie moseyed over to them. Gracie noticed that every item of clothing on his body, cap included, needed a couple of wash cycles, but it didn't take Sherlock Holmes to deduce this. Chuckie was so scrawny he looked taller than he was. He carried his skateboard under his arm.

He stopped a few yards away. "Yeah?"

"We're trying to find out where Mrs.

Parks's cat went Thursday morning. Can you help us?" Rocky's tone of voice was friendly but had an edge of command.

Gracie tried to read the boy's face and she could not. He seemed vaguely intrigued. Or was it wariness? "What's it look like?"

"Orange with dark stripes. Real Halloweenish."

Chuckie stared at the editor for a moment. Or perhaps, it would be better said that he stared through him. "Down around Billingsly's creek. Y'know, that big open field where they're gonna build the factory? I seen a cat like that around there a couple times."

"And a cute little dog about this big?" Marge held her hands in a Shih Tzu shape.

"Yeah. Angela gives the mutt dog treats sometimes, y'know? If she's outside. Gives 'em both dog treats, the cat too."

"Angela. That's Frank's daughter?" Rocky asked.

"Yeah."

"I've seen her with her father," Rocky nodded. "She's a pretty girl."

Chuckie almost looked pleased. Almost.

Rocky dug into his pocket and pulled out a dollar. "I've got no ice cream left myself, but maybe now you'd like to get yourself some. Here." He extended the bill toward

Chuckie. His voice took on a conspiratorial tone. "Sounds like you might know more about this factory business than I do. Anything you can tell the press at this time?"

"The press?"

"I run the *Mason County Gazette* when I'm not out chasing after cats."

"Oh. Uh, no, don't think so, except Frank don't want it and they're really pestering him, y'know? He says he'll ruin his land with arsenic before he'll let them cover it with asphalt. He says the paper thinks it's a good idea, y'know? So he's all like down on the paper."

"Lots of people are. That's nothing new. But, arsenic? I don't understand."

"There was this factory out on the west coast somewhere, y'know? Its smokestack put out arsenic all over the neighborhood. Took 'em years to clean it up, y'know, and the whole area was polluted majorly. That's what he's talking about. He must have told me all about it half a dozen times, y'know? He says all factories do that, but they only catch a few of 'em in the act."

"Mm. This is all news to me. What do you think?"

Gracie liked the way Rocky emphasized the *you*. And she realized too that she was watching an old pro in action, drawing information by the bucketful from a person who probably considered communicating with anyone outside his peer group to be a disgrace, if not potentially fatal.

She also perceived that the feckless Chuckie Moon had never before been asked to express his opinion. The novelty of it left him speechless, but only for the briefest moment. "I think he oughta take the money and run. I mean, y'know? It's gonna happen, so why not rake the bucks while you can, y'know?"

"Logical," Rocky nodded sagely. "And practical. He probably doesn't listen to you, though, does he."

"I'm not telling him what I think, y'know? Not as hot under the collar as he gets about it."

"And not if you're interested in his daughter."

"You got it."

"Appreciate your help, Chuckie. Thanks for stopping by to talk to us. We'll go looking down by the creek."

"No problem." Chuckie started to turn away, then stopped and turned back. He looked at Gracie. "Your cat — that big orange and black cat, y'know? — chases sheep, you know that? I seen him."

"Chases sheep! I never imagined."

"Acts more like a dog than a dog does. S'long." And he ambled away.

Rocky stared at the shock of green hair departing. "Chases sheep, huh? I wonder if farmer Frank Billingsly might not object pretty strenuously to that."

17

Gracie pulled Fannie May into the third slot from the end on the east side of the church's parking lot. As she got out, she paused to ponder one of life's interesting little questions. She found intriguing the ways in which people, herself included, exercise territorialism.

For example, she always parked in this spot. However, there were only three other cars in the lot, this being late on a Monday afternoon, and she could have parked right next to the door. But no. She obviously would rather walk the extra distance than park in someone else's pre-ordained space. This was her place — assigned from time immemorial, no doubt.

She saw that Lester Twomley was here, too. She probably would not have recognized the little sedan as being his, but she knew it was parked in "his" slot, also quite a distance from the door. The church secretary's car was parked in the slot stenciled

SECRETARY, but even if it was not marked, Gracie decided, the woman would surely park there and only there anyway.

She lifted her freshly laundered choir robe out, draped it over her arm, and headed for the front doors.

The church seemed unusually quiet today. To her, it felt a little forlorn. Yet, normally, it opened its arms and heart to her, so to speak. Whenever she entered, she felt warmly comfortable and embraced by it.

She stopped by the office to greet Pat Allen, the secretary — more to hear a human voice than to say hello — but Pat wasn't at her desk. She wasn't in the library either. With her hopes of hearing a friendly sound left unsatisfied, Gracie abandoned the quest and headed to the vestry.

It felt just as sad, somehow, as the rest of the building. It certainly seemed bigger when the choir was not in it. The melancholy silence weighed heavily. As Gracie hung her robe, the wire hanger gritched against the pole, *gggg*. Normally a sound one didn't notice, today it grated against her ear. She closed the door behind her, click. Her footfalls, running shoes on the hall carpet, made no noise.

"Gracie! Wait!"

She jumped.

Lester's voice reverberated. "I want to show you something!"

Gracie turned to watch as he came down the hall.

He stopped beside her. "How's your cat doing?"

"About the same. Thank you for asking."

"And that plan of yours, the one you were mentioning at the end of the supper, to trace where he had been, did that work out at all?"

"We followed his path as far as Porter Avenue, and people have seen him down by Willow Reach, that little creek near Frank Billingsly's. But we didn't find much, not as far as clues or any possible poisoning goes."

"Interesting. Very interesting. Come out to the parking lot, please." He headed toward the front doors. Reaching his truck, Lester hung half in and half out of the passenger side. He was rooting through his glove compartment. With a happy grin, he stood up and slammed his door. Waving a roadmap triumphantly, he beckoned.

"When Don said he was going to research toxicology reports," he explained excitedly, "that got me thinking. So I got out my county map." Lester unfolded his map across his truck's hood. The breeze grabbed a corner and tried to thwart his efforts. He held one side down, so Gracie politely held the other.

He pointed with his free hand. "I marked the locations where people reported illness. They are all marked X here. Here's where Pete Murphy lives. His dog died. Here's Mrs. Benton, whose black cat got sick. Here're you and Marge. Billingsly's sheep died here. I called all the vets in this part of the county to see if they could add anything. Turns out there've been several mysterious illnesses and one death. I don't have exact addresses, of course. But I found out the general areas. So I indicated them with O's."

With a red highlighter, Lester had drawn several irregular circles on his map. "Basically, they're all in this neighborhood where you see these rings. Porter to Graham Road to Third. When you backtracked your cat, you entered the circle here." He pointed again.

Gracie's neighborhood, almost.

"You'll notice," he continued, "that there are a few outside that circle; these two here, for example. They could be random illnesses unrelated to the problem under investigation. In fact, probably one or more inside the circle are random also. But the pattern is there. You can see it."

Gracie nodded. "You're right. And even though my house is on the edge, Gooseberry roamed through the middle of it. And Marge's dog, Charlotte. They were together, we've found out."

Lester began folding the map, obviously pleased with himself.

Gracie thought about his map and the main red circle. "Whatever it is, if it's accessible to sheep and housepets, it's probably in that principal area."

"Accessible to sheep is the key. Unlike dogs and cats, they are confined inside the fence." He waved it at her for emphasis. "I drew the circle large, but it might in truth be very tiny, the real ground zero lying somewhere inside the larger circle."

"Somewhere inside a sheep pasture," Gracie supplied. "Lester, what would I look for?"

"I don't know, I'm not a chemist. I think we should go find Don and take a drive out there to look around. Take samples, perhaps." He unfolded his map and started over. "Don is here, too, you know. He's down in the basement trying to round up a few more copies of 'Mighty Fortress.' We're short several."

"You mean, go out looking right now?"

"As good a time as any. I'm going to have to go back inside and call the auto club anyway." He grimaced, pointing to his front seat. "I seem to have just locked my keys in my truck."

18

Such a pretty little rill, this Willow Reach of Mason Creek. Gracie slid down out of the front passenger seat of Don Delano's van. She closed the door and walked across the grassy strip that led into the cool darkness of woodland.

The strip of trees bordering the road gave way almost immediately to the creek bank. Beyond the low brush and tall reeds of the creek bank, gray water poured lazily along, barely moving, satin smooth. Gracie could just so see the sheep pasture beyond the trees lining the far side.

Suddenly she heard a sound of bottles rattling. She turned to see that Don had just slung a long-handled tote from his shoulder. Collecting bottles, no doubt. Lester followed him.

Fishermen had cut numerous paths from a trail alongside the stream down to the water's edge. Carefully, lest she slip in the dirt, Gracie made her way down one of them to where the water met the land. The trees and scraggly bushes embraced her, closing in protectively behind her, then opening up before her. She stopped in the soft dirt at water's edge.

Downstream a few feet, something plopped into the water as she approached — a frog, most likely. Just upstream, a large bird lifted away with huge, noisy wing beats. Dragging its legs behind, it flapped away around a bend and out of sight.

Gracie listened to the lovely stillness a few moments. It was a different kind of silence from the heaviness in the church, a silence that somehow belonged here. Then a meadowlark cut loose out across the creek somewhere, singing counterpoint to the silence.

Enough daydreaming! There were things to be learned here. "This is the problem I've had all day, Don. Am I seeing a clue and failing to recognize it?"

"If you're missing something, so am I. I don't see anything out of the ordinary." Lester stepped in beside her. "Do we know which pasture those sheep were in?"

"Let's just check everything along the creek." Don started off along the creekside path, his collecting bag rattling. Gracie scrambled back up the bank to the path and followed. Lester crashed and rattled along behind them. Apparently, he was not a woodsman.

The leafy canopy opened up overhead, letting the weeds along the path grow lanker, waist high. The ground turned mushy beneath Gracie's feet and squooshed up around the sides of her shoes. She saw the sharp grooves where a bicycle had cut tracks in the mud. They sloshed past cattails. She resigned herself to the sure fact that her shoes would never really get clean again. The rich mud soup made footing treacherous.

Don stopped so suddenly, Gracie nearly bumped into him.

Don pointed. "Something up ahead."

Gracie listened a moment to rustling on the trail beyond Don. "It's probably a dog."

Lester frowned. "How do you know?"

"Well, I know it's not a cat, at least," she replied simply.

Don moved forward cautiously, following the noise of something moving in leaves.

The ground grew firmer; they left the cattails behind. A mound of brambles rose up beside the trail just ahead. The rustling came from beneath it.

Don knelt down, laid his collecting bag aside, and peered in. "She's right. It's a dog.

No collar." He slipped his arm in beneath the tangled mound. He yanked it back out as a creature snarled from inside.

Gracie dropped down to her knees and put her ear nearly to the ground. Now these good jeans she was wearing would never come fully clean again either.

Deep inside the tangle, on a bed of painfully sharp little blackberry leaves, a tan cocker spaniel growled again. It looked purebred or nearly so, which suggested that it belonged to someone.

"Come honey," Gracie said. "It's safe. Come to me."

"No, Gracie!" Don stood up. "Don't do that! It's sick. Don't let him bite you."

"He won't bite me. Come, poor thing. Come on out. Let us help you."

The leaves rustled. It was squirming closer. It stopped.

Gracie waited. "Don't you guys have to go find clues or something?"

Behind Gracie, Lester chuckled. "I do believe we've been thrown over for a cur. Women are so fickle." He continued up the path.

Don grunted and followed him reluctantly. "Don't forget to call us when it takes your arm off."

But Gracie was good at waiting for animals. She crooned gentle words now and then, comforting words. The dog moved a bit closer in a few moments. And then another inch. Quietly, slowly, Gracie extended her hand, knuckles forward. Don was right, of course. A sick or injured dog is more likely to savage you than lick you.

She felt its breath on the back of her hand, barely heard the sniffing. A coarse, dry tongue stroked across her knuckles. Slowly and carefully, she slipped her hand under its breast — a very thin and bony breast — and drew it toward her. It allowed her to move it. In a moment or two, she picked it out of the thicket into her arms.

It struggled briefly, then pressed in under her arms, letting her wrap around it, letting her hold it ever so gently.

"You're used to depending on people, aren't you. You haven't been a stray for very long."

The dog had, however, been a stray long enough for its unkempt coat to become matted and muddied. Beggarticks and burs had buried themselves to the skin. They would have to be clipped out. In fact the whole dog would have to be clipped. There was no way these tangles could ever be combed smooth. It was a lovely little dog, too, with silky, apricot-colored fur.

Clusters of ticks crowded together inside its huge, floppy ears. Two kinds of ticks, in fact — the soft, bulbous ones and the little hard seed ticks. The cocker's eyes drifted shut.

Gracie's nose started running and her eyes burned with tears. This could just as easily be her poor Gooseberry, friendless and alone somewhere, so ill as to be unable to make it back home. How many other pets, cut off from human nurturing, were dying out here of this mysterious malady?

She struggled to her feet, the dog cradled firmly in her arms, and continued up the trail in the direction the men had taken. She would ask Don to break off the search now and drive her back. She would carry her new charge directly to Dave Wilkins and let the lady work her medical magic.

She saw Don and Lester up ahead. On the muddy creek bank, Don was waving an arm back and forth, his finger outstretched, obviously explaining something. Lester was nodding.

Gracie quickened her pace and joined them. "What's that smell?"

Lester glanced down to the creek at his feet.

An unmistakably dead turtle lay bottom side up at water's edge.

Don looked for a moment at the dog. "Cute pup. I want to go on up this way a little further. Then we'll take that dog back. I assume you want to take it to the vet's."

Lester said, "Our local veterinarians should be getting pretty good at treating this, whatever it is. They're getting enough practice." He headed up the trail behind Don.

Gracie fell in behind them. The dog squirmed a bit, so she shifted the way she held him. She didn't want its weight on her arms mashing those sharp burs deeper into its skin.

"Here." Don crashed down through brush to water's edge.

Gracie had half a mind just to wait for them. But her "healthy" curiosity got the better of her and she struggled down to the shore. She saw several small fish floating, as well as a decomposing frog. And the more she looked, the more she saw.

"Oh, dear." She shook her head sadly. "All this hungry little dog would have to do is lick a fish or something, and it could be poisoned secondhand. If you know what I mean." She glanced again at the death and decay along the shore. "This is terrible. Can you tell anything?"

Don nestled his collecting bag into a tuft

of tall grass. "No. Not yet. I can't smell anything — other than dead fish, that is. I want to get some samples. It won't take long. Then we'll take that dog back."

Quickly, expertly, Don filled a sample bottle from some still water among a tuft of grass. He sniffed it briefly before he stoppered it. "Think I'll gather some of the mud too." He handed several vials to Lester. "Let's get some water samples from, say, about ten feet apart along the shore, in close to the bank rather than out in the current. Careful, don't fall in."

Lester knelt on the shore a bit uncertainly. He grasped the branch of a bush to steady himself. Leaning over and stretching as far as he could, he filled the vial with water from close to the bank.

Then, without warning, he tumbled over. "Help!" he shouted.

19

From in front of All Creatures, where she'd dropped off the spaniel, Gracie waved her thanks to Don, who'd followed her there and waited for her to finish. What had started as a quick errand to drop her robe off at the church had certainly turned into an event-filled excursion. She hoped the pretty little dog was going to make it. She also hoped Lester was finally warming up after getting so chilled. Only when they'd dropped him at his house had his teeth finally stopped chattering.

Since there was still an hour or so before Uncle Miltie would expect her home, she wanted to return to the creek where she and the men had just been exploring. Might there be something to find on the other shore, the "sheep side," so to speak?

As she drove back out to Willow Reach, instead of turning aside onto County Road 17, she continued up to the cement bridge across the reach. She was now a quarter mile from where they had just been exploring, but from here she could walk along the creek bank on the other shore.

She locked her car up and carefully picked her way down the slope into the roadside ditch. To her right, the creek gurgled as it drew its shoulders together to squeeze through the culvert beneath the road.

She figured out right away that she was not nearly as fast at climbing fences as she used to be. It took her a while to hoist herself up one side of the fence, get a leg on the other side without snagging her jeans on the top strand of barbed wire, and then let herself down inside the field.

Almost immediately, she realized that maybe this wasn't quite as great an idea as it had first appeared. On Frank Billingsly's side of the creek, no fishermen's path helped you reach the water's edge. Tangles of trees, weeds, bushes, thistles and brambles clogged the shore between the close-clipped pasture and the creek.

She faced two choices, both unpleasant: walk out in the meadow and not be anywhere close to the water, or fight the impossible jungle every step of the way. Besides, the creek bank sloped more steeply on this side than on the other. If she wasn't very careful, she would follow poor Lester into the drink.

She battled weeds valiantly for all of twenty feet before the weeds won. It was easier to make her way away from the creek, up into the open meadow. Slowed down because a prickly vine tangled itself around her ankle, she eventually emerged beyond the trees and bushes and, moments later, was walking freely along the side of the open field.

As far as she knew, Gooseberry didn't ever go this far down to the creek's edge. Even if he had been prowling the sheep pasture and accepting treats from Frank's daughter, he'd never come home wet.

It all looked so *ordinary.*

Did sheep ever graze here? The grass was nibbled very closely. Gracie knew that sheep did that. But was this the sheep pasture in question? For that matter, were Frank's sheep in the pasture when they were afflicted? She really ought to simply go up to his house and ask him. Stumbling around out here in the great outdoors wasn't telling her anything; it merely raised more questions.

She turned around to return to her car, then changed her mind. The Billingsly place sat perched on the breast of this hill less than half a mile from this spot. Many's the morning she walked eight times that far for no other reason than to get out and walk. She would cross the pasture and see if Frank was home. That way, she could ask him all her questions directly.

She took off at a smart walk along the smooth curve of the hillside, angling casually upward, gaining just a wee bit of elevation with each stride.

Now that she had left the creek and climbed somewhat, she could see across to the open space beyond the creek where the trees temporarily parted, very near where they'd found the dog. She could almost make out the pile of brambles under which the little pooch had hidden. It made her pause and wonder how her own Gooseberry fared.

What was this? She stopped, squinting for just a bit clearer resolution. It looked like Jeffrey Larson, pedaling a bicycle along the creekside trail. And behind him, also on a bike, a much smaller child struggled to keep up. They were hastening toward the main road, bumpety-bumping on the track. They disappeared beyond the trees. Puzzled and unsure of her observation, she returned to her trek.

A meadowlark flew up in front of her, a

blur of bright yellow and drab grey-brown. It set its wings and coasted to a fence post at the top of the hill. Delightful!

There sat Frank's farm on the hillcrest ahead. She hadn't far to go now. She wondered how he was doing with his new chickens. He used to keep them in a henhouse downhill of the barn. As she drew closer she could see that the henhouse was still there, still surrounded by its high poultry-netting fence.

A person was moving around inside the chicken yard. And she didn't have to wonder about her eyesight on this one: You could probably spot that green hair from a mile away. Apparently Frank had finally wangled some work out of the swain Chuckie; he must be in there feeding the chickens.

The birds had begun squawking. This close, Gracie could see them clearly as they scurried wildly about and burst into the air on stubby wings. Amid the turmoil, some of the most panicked ones made it over the top of the fence. Still squawking, the escapees fluttered and flapped down the hill. Chuckie was flailing something. It looked like a broom or shovel. At that moment, she heard the familiar, staggering motor in Frank Billingsly's ancient pickup truck.

The motor died, coughing.

"Hey!" Frank's voice roared nearly louder than his truck ever sounded.

Chuckie paused.

She could hear the voices raised in argument, but she couldn't make out words specifically. She didn't want to. She stopped. Should she continue forward or just quietly go away? Either option could prove embarrassing. To appear in the midst of an argument is discomfiting to all concerned. On the other hand, what if Frank saw her leaving and thought she was somehow connected to Chuckie?

With no good choices, Gracie resigned herself to embarrassment in any case and continued forward toward the farmyard.

Frank and Chuckie now had switched positions; Frank, who'd been at the gate, stood inside the chicken yard. Chuckie was nearer the gate, waving his arms and yelling furiously. Suddenly, he ducked outside and slammed the gate, sprinting away. As Frank stood shaking his fist, Chuckie's car engine roared. Gravel sprayed the driveway as the green-haired boy sped away from the Billingsly farmyard.

Feeling weary, Gracie climbed the last bit of pasture hillside. Frank saw her, of course. If he thought it odd that she was strolling across his sheep pasture, he didn't show it. Maybe he was just too mad at Chuckie to pay much attention to the strangeness of it.

She stepped up to the fence and smiled wanly. "I seem to have dropped by at a bad time."

20

Frank stood in his disrupted chicken yard watching the farm lane a few moments. From where she stood, Gracie was unable to see Chuckie's leavetaking, but she could certainly follow it by ear. She slogged the final few yards to the fence separating Frank's yard from his sheep pasture.

With the wave of an arm, he gestured toward the way in. "Gate over there."

By the time she reached it, Frank was there to open it for her. "I was gonna make a pot of coffee."

"I'd like that." Gracie followed him to the house.

They stomped up the back stoop, Gracie being old enough to know that the stomping was to shake loose dirt off your feet. The long spring on the old wooden-frame screen door sagged. It did the job though, drawing the door closed after Gracie passed through.

In the Billingslys' kitchen, only one small

window let sunshine in. No curtains, no doo-dads or memorabilia. But it was clean and quiet and well kept, and that made it inviting to her. She settled into a harp-back wooden chair at a full-sized table by the only window.

Frank fumbled in a cabinet for filters. "If I wasn't so blamed mad, I'd stop to wonder why you're hoofing it across my pasture field."

"And I'll be happy to explain. What was Chuckie Moon trying to do?!"

"I don't know. Kill my chickens. Or else get 'em so upset they quit laying." Frank scooped ample coffee into the pot. "You heard the ranting. You know as much as I do."

"But I couldn't make out words. I could see the anger, though."

"That's right. Anger. It's what the kid's built out of." He paused, his head twisted awry as he watched the coffee maker begin its gurgle-and-drip. "Don't know how Angie got mixed up with him in the first place."

How much should Gracie contribute to this discussion? She wasn't certain. Neither was she sure that this was the time to exercise caution. "As I understand it, their friendship was not entirely Angie's idea.

142

And she was too kind-hearted to turn Chuckie down or break it off immediately."

Frank stared at her a moment. Shaking his head, he came over to the table. "Somebody told me once that you hear everything, but that one beats the drum. You're even up on high school romances."

"I may have already said too much."

Frank sighed and stared at his elderly refrigerator a few moments. "Mildred's in Florida. She generally goes down there to visit her parents in winter, but her dad's heart isn't good and her mom's getting dizzy spells. She figured she oughta go down now because she might have to put them in a care facility of some kind. Angie and I — we don't know how to talk to each other. Know what I mean?"

"A blessing on your in-laws. I'll keep them in prayer."

"Thanks. Anyway, Mildred and Angie really understand each other. Me, I understand chickens." He leaned across the table. "Gracie, I got a huge favor to ask you. I still don't know why you were galloping across my pasture, but I don't care. I'm thinking God just delivered you when I need you. I'm thinking you — being a woman as you are, y'know? — might be able to talk to Angie like I can't. With Mildred out of town and this Chuckie business blowing up in my face, I'm at my wit's end. I just can't figure out what's going on! What if he decides to burn my barn or something? Can you help me?"

What could she say? Her brain screamed, *No! No! Don't get involved in this! Stay out of there!* even as her heart was taking charge of her vocal cords and making her say, "Of course, I'll try to help. I don't know how much good I can do."

"Just find out what's going on would be a big help." And this philosopher-farmer who understood chickens looked absolutely stricken. He poured the coffee then, and they began to discuss other subjects.

Suddenly, from out in front of the house came the noise of a large motor in serious trouble, accompanied by a mighty grinding sound.

Gracie teased. "Don't tell me they haven't thrown away the yellow Sasquatch yet!"

Frank smiled. "Nope. And I bet you can tell from the squealing they can't fix the brakes right on it. Bobby says he takes it into the bus barn about every week for them to work on it some more. The repair costs would have paid for a new one three times over. At least they only use it as the late bus for the athletic teams."

"They don't actually take our teams out of town in it, do they?"

"Criminy no! They'd just have to send another bus out to get our kids home again. It's the biggest piece of junk in the state."

The front door slammed. "Dad? I'm home."

"Angie!" Frank shouted. "Come in here a minute, please."

Moments later, Angie appeared in the kitchen doorway still wearing her basketball uniform, her gym bag over her shoulder. When Rocky called her a pretty girl, he was right — once you looked. Her body was slim, virtually without curves, and her face plain. Her brown hair hung rather limply. Pretty physically? Not exactly. But the sweetness that showed through more than made up for any plainness of features. Here was a child beautiful on the inside, and that beauty cannot be masked or hidden.

"Hi, Mrs. Parks." She looked surprised for only a moment. Then a light dawned. "Oh, so that's your car parked down by the creek. Out walking?"

"As a matter of fact, yes. Good afternoon, Angie. Who won?"

Angie smiled. "The coach, I guess. It was practice."

Frank abruptly stood up. "Mrs. Parks

145

wants to talk to you, so talk to her, all right? I have to feed the chickens." The screen door slammed behind him.

Angie looked at Gracie suspiciously. "What do you want to talk about?"

"Well, Chuckie Moon. He seems to be very angry about something, and we hoped you might be able to shed some light."

"He's always angry. Look, uh, I'm sorry to sound unfriendly, but I have a lot of home-work tonight."

"Do you make dinner for your father and brother while your mother's in Florida?"

"Usually."

Gracie bounded to her feet. "Good! Let's put this time to good use and get it ready to-gether. Do you know what you're going to have?"

"Whatever's in the fridge, I guess." Angie dropped her bag by the doorway. Gracie watched over her shoulder as she peered in-side for inspiration. Someone liked pickles; Gracie counted four opened jars. Egg car-tons, not surprisingly, were in abundance.

Angie yanked the meat keeper open. "We have some sausage."

"Do you have spaghetti?"

"Yeah, but no spaghetti sauce. We're out of that too." Angie stood up straight.

"How about tomato sauce?"

"I think so." Angie opened a cabinet. "No tomato paste, though."

Gracie noticed a bottle of vinegar on the shelf. "I believe I saw lettuce in the crisper. And some garlic in that hanging basket."

"But we ran out of salad dressing yesterday."

Gracie, noticing a stale loaf of bread, calculated for a brief moment. "How about spaghetti with sausage sauce, garlic bread and a salad with vinaigrette dressing?"

Angie frowned. "You mean make spaghetti sauce and salad dressing from scratch?" Then she shrugged. "I can't think of anything else."

Gracie rubbed her hands together gleefully. "I love to cook. I suppose you knew that."

Angie grinned. "Sure, you cater stuff sometimes. I'd like to if I had more time." She went over to the sink to wash her hands.

So did Gracie. "The most boring class I ever took in high school was home economics, but I had to take it. It was required for all the girls. I wanted to learn how to make aspics and fancy omelets and angel food cakes. Instead, we made scrambled eggs. I wanted to do *real* cooking!"

"We don't have to take home ec now. It's not required." Angie handed the towel to

Gracie. "Most of us girls, we could use it. But with sports and stuff, we just don't get to it."

"Girls, and boys as well! Boys should know how to cook and mend clothes, too. I'm all in favor of home ec for boys." Gracie started setting out ingredients — the vinegar and oil for the salad dressing, tomato sauce, the half loaf of bread.

For the next ten minutes they talked about "safe" things. Gracie learned all about boys' resistance to anything remotely domestic, and girls' resistance to being stuck behind an apron. She learned about the sports program and what it still needed to achieve true greatness.

Then, somehow, the conversation switched to the social scene. Gracie learned quickly that all the rituals of dating hadn't changed that much over the years. They had only become more complicated — or so it seemed.

Finally, she took the plunge and asked, "What did you see in Chuckie Moon? I know he has his good points."

And Angie, apparently swept up in the unknown pleasure of making spaghetti sauce from scratch, did not become defensive or close down. "When should we start the water for the spaghetti? Chuckie's good points? I don't know, exactly. He pays attention to you. He listens, and he gets jealous. He makes you feel like he really cares about you."

"We could start it now. Here, get a spoon and taste. Can you tell how the flavors are starting to marry? I heard, and I'm not going to say where, that going together was more his idea than yours."

"Yeah, I guess so." Angie pulled a large wooden spoon from the flatware drawer. "He just kept insisting until I went out with him. And now he thinks I should be his forever." She dipped the spoon into the pan, blew on it a moment, and tasted. The sweetest smile spread across her face. "This is better than out of a jar! They're going to love this!"

"What are you going to do about it? About Chuckie, I mean. Do you know yet?"

Angie began to fill a pot with water. "I already did, sort of. I told him I didn't want to go out as much. He got mad and said some nasty things. So I told him it wasn't really me, but it was my dad who didn't want me going out so much."

"Are you frightened of him?"

Angie paused. "Yeah. I guess I am. He talks about all the stuff he's learned in chemistry. He showed me a penny once that he soaked in acid a little while, and it evaporated down to this real thin, real shiny little thing smaller than a dime. That's scary, huh? And then he says, 'Imagine that on your skin.' Gross!"

21

Gracie's beloved El, the husband who'd died way before she was ready to let him go, had claimed there should be a law against computers. Right before his accident, he'd added cell phones to the proscribed list. At times, Gracie was not so sure that he hadn't been right. Computers operate in a Through-the-Looking-Glass universe and obviously delight in thwarting and befuddling intruders into their mystifying world.

Don Delano had entered that wonderland universe this evening. But, then, Gracie knew he often trespassed there and had adjusted to the rules.

She was perched on a stool in the high school's chemistry lab, just behind Don Delano's right shoulder. Behind his other one, Rocky Gravino sat.

She watched as Don swirled his mouse about, now and then typing in a phrase. He was surfing the Web, something Gracie thought she never intended to do in this life.

Suddenly Rocky grunted. A glitch! If automobiles had breakdown records as poor as a computer's, they'd all be recalled. Why, she wondered, did people put up with it?

Don muttered something, then raised his voice. "Wait a minute. I think we have something. There it is."

The screen flicked through a series of pictures. A photo of a very tall cylindrical smokestack painted itself down the screen.

Gracie leaned forward to read the screen better. "Asarco Smelter. That's the arsenic pollution Chuckie says Frank Billingsly talked about?"

Don nodded. "Tacoma, Washington. It operated many years, and arsenic was one of the by-products. But that situation is nothing at all like ours. Metallurgy has its own chemistry, and the proposed parts factory would be totally different."

Rocky sat up straight and stretched his back. "So what was Frank Billingsly piping off about?"

"Well," Don abandoned his mouse, leaning back in his chair. "You're familiar with the term *poison pill*."

Rocky frowned. "You mean the situation when a little company is about to be taken over by a big company in a hostile takeover, and it does something that would make it-self undesirable?"

"Yeah. Like take on a big debt quickly or something." Don looked at them. "Buying or leasing land for a factory is a business deal. A very big business deal," he explained.

"Let's say Frank doesn't want to part with his land, but he's tired of fighting the company. Even more likely, he's afraid he might lose. So he makes that land suddenly undesirable. Faced with a huge outlay of capital, the company looks elsewhere, and Frank's land lies fallow and un-paved-over, safe from the corporate monster. You think he might do that?"

Rocky's face softened. "Poison it with a pollutant. Force them either to spend a fortune cleaning it up or to look for a site elsewhere. Even if his property was number one on their hit parade, they'd abandon it. You know, it has a nice ring to it, Don."

Don waved at the screen. "Look how many millions of dollars Asarco shelled out. That's a lot of bucks to pay a cleaning lady."

Gracie gasped. "Oh, I'm sure Frank isn't like that at all!"

Rocky shook his head. "There's gotta be a law against that. They'd nail him to his own barn door."

"Not if they don't suspect him." Don was getting excited, Gracie could tell. "Whose sheep died first? Frank's. Nobody's going to put him in the suspect category. He's already been placed in the victim category."

"Yeah," Rocky agreed. "Yeah! The price of a couple sheep is pretty cheap insurance, when you come right down to it. And here's another kink: Sheep are big animals. They dropped dead. And yet, small animals, like Gracie's cat or Marge's dog — or that cocker spaniel you guys found — did not die. The small animals should have died quicker than sheep because their body size is less. Same as it takes less poison to kill a child than an adult."

Don nodded. "Although different animals have different sensitivities."

"You mean, for instance," Gracie added, "like you never feed chocolate to a dog. It makes them sick but it doesn't affect human beings, except the ones with allergies."

"Right." Don sat forward, propped his wire-rimmed glasses at an angle to best see the screen, and began typing rapidly. The phrase "sheep illnesses" tracked across the search bar. He sat back. "Let's see if there's anything a sheep man should be especially careful to protect sheep from."

The newspaperman crossed his arms.

"We keep talking about ingesting something, but that's not the only way you can get poisoned. What if it's something that's absorbed through the skin, or the lungs? It could just lie on the ground. The victim picks it up in passing. Or sniffs the poison into its nostrils incidentally as it's sniffing at something else."

"Or while grazing."

Rocky leaned past Gracie to see the computer screen better. "I mean, your average dog is too smart to eat poison deliberately. Cats, maybe. But not a dog."

"Whoa!" Both Don and Gracie looked accusingly at their companion. "Dogs are smarter than cats? I don't think so. Your average cat can repair a computer with a fork. Your average dog can't find the fork."

Don, Gracie knew, was owned by Oscar, a white ball of fluff with a little pink nose sticking out the front end.

Rocky reminded them, "I suppose if you get lost in the Alps, you can expect a tabby to show up with a cask of brandy. And how many Siamese can herd a flock of a thousand sheep single-handed? And do police pussycats sniff out bombs and drug smugglers? Get real, Delano."

Rocky, of course, was a dog person.

"Dogs," Don continued, "do poorly on

intelligence tests. Cats are too smart to take the tests. Dogs are high maintenance. You can go away for a couple days and your cat very nicely will take care of itself in your absence. Let's see you leave a dog to its own devices for a long weekend."

Enough of this. Gracie slid off her stool. "Yesterday I explored the woods, today the Internet. I'm *tired*. Good night, gentlemen."

As she stepped out the double doors into the twilight, the evening felt soft and smelled sweet. She really ought to head home and rest before eating with Uncle Miltie. But when she started the car, she drove not to her house but to Dave Wilkins's veterinary office. She pulled into the parking area out front and walked to the door.

It was silly. The office was surely closed now. After all, there were the hours of business posted on the door. On the other hand, a light burned halfway back on the east side of the building. It drew her as it would draw a moth.

A sidewalk led to the rear of the building, where a door said "Private." Nonetheless, she turned the knob. It opened, so she stepped inside.

A girl in a blond ponytail was sweeping in the hallway. She smiled at Gracie. "Hi.

You're Gooseberry's mom, aren't you? And you and that teacher brought in the apricot cocker yesterday."

"Yes. You're not closed?"

"The office is closed. We clean after hours. I won't be locking it down for five or ten minutes yet, though I did lock the hall where the dogs are. Do you want to go visit Charlotte and Gent?"

"Gent? The cocker spaniel?"

The girl smiled as she nodded. "You know the old Disney cartoon, *Lady and the Tramp*? He looks a lot like Lady — but he's *not* one. So we call him Gent. Anyway, I'll go unlock the hall again if you want to go see them."

"No need for that. I just dropped by, thinking about Gooseberry."

The girl dipped her head toward the far end of the hall. "You're welcome to go say good night to him."

"Has the doctor figured out what's making him sick?"

The girl shook her head. "Ran all kinds of tests. Nothing yet. But she'll keep trying."

"I know she will. Thank you." Gracie took her time walking down the hall toward the quiet room. For some reason, she felt reluctant to go there. Apprehensive. And that was silly. She opened the door and stepped inside.

She waited for her eyes to adjust to the gentle glow of a night light on one side of the room and a digital clock on the other. It smelled like animals in here, though certainly not like animal wastes. The staff kept the place scrupulously clean, obviously. But animals — well, they smell like animals, warm and vaguely sweet.

Gooseberry's cage sported his name, hand-lettered on a piece of tag board.

Gracie crossed to it and opened his door. "Gooseberry?" She heard stirring. She could not see into the low cage. It was much too dark. She knew Gooseberry with his cat eyes could see out, though, so she bent low, her face at the door, that he might look at her if he so chose. She reached into the blackness, felt the dark wool blanket he was lying on, felt the familiar thick fur, felt the sensitive little ears.

He moved a bit beneath her fingers. Not much. When she laid her hand on him, she could discern vertebrae by touch. He was losing a lot of weight fast. She scratched behind his ears because she knew he loved that. She scratched under his chin because he loved that next best. She rubbed the tiny chest. It did not vibrate. No purr tonight.

For several minutes she simply stroked the soft curved back, over and over and over, as she had done so many times through the years.

Lord, please help Gooseberry and use me to get to the bottom of all these goings-on. And, silently, because it was the quiet room, she wept.

22

The *Mason County Gazette* lay open on the kitchen counter. Gracie could find nothing in it about anything even vaguely to do with dead sheep or sick animals of any kind.

She mulled the mystery of Rocky's silence on the subject as she went back to her bacon, mushroom and cheese omelet. Behind her the tabletop kitchen TV blared out the morning news as Uncle Miltie finished his own breakfast. He was not a newspaper person.

Rocky's omission of any mention of their findings and theories intrigued her. He knew what was going on. Indeed, he'd gone out of his way to investigate. Too, he prided himself that he and his small staff stayed on top of breaking stories. The *Mason County Gazette* routinely published all the dirt even in advance of the rumor mills, and in a town this size, that was saying something.

The phone rang as she was carrying her empty plate to the sink.

"Hello." Automatically, Gracie wedged the phone against her shoulder to free both hands.

"Good morning. Paul Meyer here. Not calling too early, am I?"

"Not at all. What can I do for you?"

"I think I mentioned I wanted to bring that scout by sometime. Dale Springer."

"Yes, I remember. When would you like to come?"

"Well, uh, is right now convenient? Or would you prefer later?"

"No, now is just fine. I look forward to meeting him." Actually, Gracie always liked to take her walk after breakfast, but as priorities go, she allowed Pastor Paul's need to take precedence.

Besides, she was becoming exceedingly curious about this mysterious person. Don, obviously, was inclined to condemn him, as were Harry and his friends, while Rocky and Paul defended him vigorously. Who was correct? Or was it not Mr. Springer at all, but simply what he represented that generated such intense reactions?

"Meet who?" Waving the remote with one hand, Uncle Miltie clicked past the commercials as he scarfed up the last of his breakfast with the other.

"The scout we've all been hearing about."

Uncle Miltie hit the mute button; the sound blared forth anew. "All that arguing. Complaining. I'm sick of him. Try to get a decent hand of cards going down at the senior center. You might as well just hide under your chair to start with, 'cause pretty soon the false teeth and spit are gonna start flying."

The doorbell rang as Gracie was closing the dishwasher door. She stood up and dried her hands off.

"Good luck," Uncle Miltie called above the din of the morning news. Gratefully, Gracie left the noise behind.

She would have invited Pastor Paul in, but he stood on the edge of the porch, paused to fly. She closed the door behind her. "Dale is headed on over to the first of a couple properties we're considering. I swung by to pick you up."

"Thank you." Gracie let him escort her to his car. "I'm still not certain exactly how I can help." He held the door as she slid into the passenger seat.

Paul sat behind the wheel. "We'd like to show you a couple of locations so that you know exactly where they are. Rumors around town are sometimes pretty inaccurate." He continued, "We want to bring you up to speed, explain what the project would do, how it would change things — and fail to change things. Give you a clear picture. Then, I hope, you can suggest ways to help alleviate people's fears about the enterprise."

"New things always frighten some people." Gracie observed that they were headed for Frank Billingsly's first.

"You never seem to be frightened of new things."

"You didn't see me when El died. On top of the hideous grief was my fear of facing life all alone. It took awhile."

He drove in silence awhile. Gracie could not tell from his expressionless face what was on his mind, but obviously, something was and he was considering it from all angles.

Just beyond the Willow Reach, they pulled onto the shoulder of the road. Paul parked within yards of where Gracie had parked two days earlier. Frank's sheep pasture stretched off across the curving hillside to their right.

From the car ahead, a slim, elegant young woman got out, her cell phone at her ear. She spoke a few words and holstered it. And Gracie felt her mouth drop open. Quickly she closed it. For also here came Jeffrey's friend, Roger, cautiously climbing out of the back seat on the road shoulder side of the car.

The young woman glanced disapprovingly at him and switched on her well-shaped smile. You could hardly tell it was artificial. She came striding over to Paul and Gracie. She was wearing a pair of those fashionable lace-up dress shoes that pretend to be sensible but aren't, really.

"Good morning, Paul."

"Good morning. Gracie, may I present Dale Springer, the scout for Auto-Mate Sales and Manufacturing."

"Delighted," said Ms. Springer. She dipped her head toward Roger. "This is my son. I'm sorry, I ordinarily never take him out on business, but it's a school holiday and his sitter called in sick."

"Good morning, Roger." Gracie smiled at the child because the boy looked very much like he needed a smile.

"Oh. You know each other."

"Through Jeffrey Larson." Gracie turned to Paul. "Jeffrey is going to chemistry camp. I trust you know that."

Paul smiled. "Yes. His parents have asked the church to sponsor him. We're bringing it up before the board." He waved an arm toward the sheep pasture. "You know this is Dale's favorite site, so far."

And the woman who was raising such a furor in Willow Bend launched almost automatically into her spiel. "Ideal location. Notice the outcrops here and there. Plenty of bedrock to build on. We'll cut a deal with the county to widen the road in from the freeway."

She pointed to the fishermen's track on the other side of the creek and beyond. "The lot extends across the creek to that abandoned road over there. We'll channelize the creek and put the employees' parking lot right over it. We'll be able to park a hundred cars there." She continued on for at least two more minutes, explaining what it would look like and extolling the virtues of Auto-Mate. Finally she paused for breath.

Gracie nodded. "I didn't hear you explain how you're going to build a flat factory on a sloping hillside. Isn't the gradient too steep?"

"That's what bulldozers are for. It will be nice and level when they're done."

Gracie tried to imagine the scene with the improvements Ms. Springer was describing. Where would the meadowlarks go? The frogs and turtles? The woodpecker and the berry brambles? Where would the killdeer nest?

When they left here, Gracie knew, they

would go on to visit other places that would need paving and channelizing and bull-dozing. They would talk about replacing meadows with cement and dreams.

It was going to be a long, long day.

23

When in the course of human events one of Immense and Pressing Importance pends, the world stops.

The world had just stopped. The event? Church clean-up day. Gracie tossed her rake, hedge-pruning shears, loppers and gloves into the back seat. She cranked the key in the ignition, hoping this session would be over with quickly, fearing it would not.

Frankly, she was getting quite tired of the way Barb and some of the others at the church ranked priorities. When it was choir, choir practice suddenly became the most important thing in the world, and don't you dare miss a single minute of rehearsal! Three or four times a year, church clean-up day showed up on the calendar.

Not too coincidentally, Barb was also in charge of that this year. So now, of course, this was the most important thing in the whole world, and don't you dare shirk your duty by failing to show up in order to be bossed around!

How Gracie wished she were curling up in her favorite chair with a fresh mystery novel or the latest issue of *Guideposts* and a cup of tea. And the still-absent Gooseberry somewhere safely and snugly nearby. Spending all day yesterday with Pastor Paul and Dale Springer had worn her to a nubbin. By midafternoon, Roger had ended up falling asleep in the backseat. Gracie, however, had not been granted that luxury.

She drove over to the church more or less automatically. Her mind was attempting not to accept Gooseberry's departure from the household as a permanent state of affairs, but as the days wore on, it was becoming increasingly difficult.

What was this? As Gracie turned into the church parking lot, she saw Rocky Gravino's car parked near the door. What in the world would the newspaper editor be doing at the church right now?

Today, she pulled not into her cosmically-assigned parking space but into the slot over in the far corner by the shrubbery. She would be tackling those bushes as her first task this morning. Why carry trimming tools all over the place when you can park them eight feet from the job?

Lester Twomley was sweeping the far lot, the one they didn't use much, with a huge push broom. Rick Harding, on his hands and knees, was using a rake to drag half-rotted leaves and twigs away from the foundation. Shoving a wheelbarrow, Don Delano disappeared around the corner, the Turner twins following behind him. Gracie sighed heavily. As always, the same twenty percent of the church's familiar faces shouldered eighty percent of the workload. Why could the burden not be distributed more evenly?

She greeted the other workers she saw, including Marybeth and Herb Bower and Amy Cantrell's best friend, Francine Barton.

Still, she couldn't stop wondering what Rocky was up to. That old healthy curiosity again. Impulsively, she laid her tools beside the bushes and walked to the front doors.

Chatter and chuckles drifted up from the kitchen, so Gracie went there. Barb stood beside the coffeepot. Beside her was Rocky, who saw Gracie approaching and smiled. "Good morning!" he boomed, his mouth only partly full of coffeecake.

"Good morning."

"I'm glad you made it." Barb said. "Did you remember to bring the hedge trimmers?

The bushes at the end of the lot are a tangled mess!"

"My first job."

Barb was determined to play the boss. "And the pear trees behind the play yard need attention desperately."

"I brought my loppers." Did Gracie want a piece of cake? She couldn't decide. "Who made the coffee?"

"Lester, I think."

Lester made pretty good coffee. Maybe Gracie would have just a slice before she got started, for once she was out there pruning and trimming, returning for cake would be inconvenient at the very least.

Barb swiveled her attention back to Rocky. "As I was saying. . . ." Gracie did not pay heed.

She retrieved the personal mug she kept stashed on the top shelf of the pantry and poured hot, inky coffee. The coffeecake and pastries had already been pretty well picked over. She should have gotten here earlier. Oh well, there was an intact doughnut.

Rocky tapped her arm. It startled her; she hadn't noticed him coming. "Come on outside a minute."

Now she would find out why he was here. Ever the newspaperman, he had obviously come wanting to learn something. But why did he always think she would know it? She was *not* a gossip, as everyone knew. She carried her coffee and doughnut along, of course.

As they approached the hall, Don came bounding in. Mud and wetness stained the knees of his jeans. "Good morning, Gracie!" He paused in front of Rocky and raised a finger. "One word. Iditarod."

"Huh?" Rocky frowned.

"No way you'd ever get eight cats to drag a sled through snow in zero weather. They're much too smart for that." And he swept on by towards the coffee table.

Gracie slowly shook her head. "You two are still embroiled in that argument? When you're so obviously wrong?"

He laughed. "I guess you're equally stubborn."

Men. Honestly. She took a bite.

They pushed out through the double doors and strolled up the sidewalk toward Gracie's car.

Rocky was studying her suspiciously. "What's wrong?"

"Nothing."

"Baloney. You're not Gracie Parks today."

"Now that is what I call news, Mr. Editor."

"Hey, I know Gracie Parks. She's effervescent. Upbeat. Always a smile."

"I'm smiling. See."

"Hmm. I repeat: What's wrong?"

She thought for a brief moment that she could keep up the façade, but common sense prevailed. She knew better. "Well, Gooseberry, for one thing. Until you pointed it out, I didn't realize I'm letting it show. I guess I am. Sorry."

"Forgiven. Of course."

Gracie waited for him to say something else. The silence quickly grew uncomfortable. And so she spoke, simply to end the irritating quiet. "I spent most of the day yesterday with Pastor Paul and the scout, exploring potential Auto-Mate factory sites. I'm not sure why, but it left me dissatisfied. I suppose *depressed* would be an even better word. Anyway, it's just a brief mood. Pay it no mind."

"So what do you think?"

"About?"

"The factory sites."

As she tried to articulate her thoughts, she realized a startling truth: She didn't have any. She had put the whole thing out of her mind the moment she got home. That must have been a deliberate ploy on her brain's part, because she normally thought through things like that very carefully.

What exactly were her thoughts, she wondered. She tried doing her thinking aloud. "I suspect it's depressing because I so much prefer the meadows and woodlots to another plant with an asphalt parking lot. I recognize that even things we love must yield to progress, and I understand that you and Paul are right. The county desperately does need the jobs it would provide. Still, it saddens me to think what we will have to lose in order to gain what it will bring."

They had arrived at her car, so she stood beside its front bumper.

Rocky brushed his hands together. "These the shrubs you're supposed to trim up? How high do you want them?"

"Window level." She was going to add, *but we certainly don't expect you to do it. You're not even a church member.* She caught herself before speaking and held her peace. This man who denied the Word and doubted God had just picked up the hedge trimmers to perform a useful service for the God whom he did not avow. She was not about to discourage him — who knew where it might lead?

She watched for a few minutes as he chopped across the tops of the bushes. With elbows splayed, he hauled away with the shears as leaves and twigs flew. His trim line was exactly even, exactly level. He had manicured more than one hedge in the past, obviously. On the other hand, he was cutting at chest level. When Gracie tried to trim the tops of these bushes, she had to work at nose level. It's a lot easier to do the job when your elbows are pointed straight out instead of projecting to either side of your ears.

Presently Rocky announced as he worked, "Your church needs electric clippers for this. Too much hedge for these wimpy little shears." *Snip snap snip.* "Do you realize you're a very powerful woman right now?"

"What do you mean?"

"Your Pastor Meyer is nobody's fool. He knows you're respected in this town as being sensible. You don't go off, grinding any axes. So if you say this factory thing's a good idea, that's gonna carry a lot of weight. More than you realize, I suspect, especially when they make their formal proposal before the council. And all you have to do is be against it, and you'll set it way back."

"Oh, hardly! I can't believe that!"

He stopped the snip-snipping to turn and look at her. "I'm not debating with you, Gracie. I'm *telling* you something you apparently aren't aware of. Whether you like it or not, you're very important to the outcome of this very proposition that upsets you."

And hearing that upset her most of all.

24

The church's windows were washed. Its shrubbery was trimmed, its leaves crushed and bagged, its pear trees pruned, its walkways swept, its front pews dusted, its array of snacks fully consumed and its clean-up crew milling in the kitchen.

Lester Twomley busied himself cleaning up the coffee maker. Barb Jennings informed her co-workers that her own yard could use a little sprucing up and no one who stopped by to help would be turned away. She left. Nobody followed. But Gracie, being Gracie, made a mental note to give her a call about it.

Then she switched tracks and asked Don, "What does it mean to channelize a stream, exactly?"

"Well, let's see. How do I explain it?" He stared at the middle pantry shelf a moment. "Okay. To get water from one place to another the quickest, you run it in a straight line. The sides and bottom of your channel, whether it's a pipe or conduit, should be as smooth and featureless as possible. Any bumps or submerged objects cause the water to eddy and lose forward speed. To channelize a stream, you bulldoze all the kinks and turns out of it. You'll probably line it with cement, too."

"Where do you keep your trashcan liners?" Rocky called to no one in particular.

"Here." Marybeth Bower dug into the cupboard under the sink to get him one.

Gracie tried to make sense of what she'd just heard. "Dale Springer was talking about channelizing the creek at Billingsly's. Why would they be so anxious to make the water flow quickly?"

"A couple of reasons. One is, if the area is prone to flooding, you want it to drain as fast as possible. The other reason is, you're someone who doesn't mind destroying the natural diversity we're going to desperately need someday, just because it's easier than learning to live with the real world."

Don shifted his attention momentarily. "Hey, Rocky, just leave that bag of trash by the steps and we'll take it out when garbage collection comes by."

Lester switched out the light over the coffee counter.

"When you channelize a creek," Don continued, "you essentially destroy it. Especially if you try to keep it dredged."

Rocky paused beside them, a very full black trash bag in hand. "You're overstating it. Water's water. Fish live in water. As long as the water's there, no problem."

"Yes, it's a problem. You'll have eighteen, twenty species of fish in a natural stream. Some live on the bottom, some prefer gravel, others live farther up in the water column and others need root tangles or eelgrass to hang out in. In other words, there are a lot of specialized little habitats in what looks like a featureless stream."

"Yes, but . . ."

Don went on, undeterred. "But the important part, of course is all the aquatic insects, mussels, amphibians, crustaceans and such that go along with it. The fish can't exist without them. All those other things need cover, too — that is, hiding places. A straight cement channel doesn't have any. The plant eaters need plants, fish and other things as well. And the crawdads, the clams and the insects need soft substrate to dig their burrows in. All gone. And without them, the fish can't make a living. That is, they can't find food."

Gracie's heart felt heavier and heavier.

Rocky dropped the trash bag by the steps. "Come on, Mrs. Parks. I'll buy you lunch."

"Thank you. I'm ready for that. My muscles have had their workout for this morning."

He raised an index finger in front of Don. "One word. Lassie."

Don frowned. "Lassie?"

"Famous movie star. Lots of famous movie stars are dogs. Rin-Tin-Tin. Benji. Lady. Tramp. You name it. How many movies star cats? Acting takes brains, Delano. So long."

Everyone said good-bye to everyone else. Gracie preceded Rocky out the door and paused on the church steps. "Which car?"

"Take yours home and I'll go pick you up?"

She waved, headed off, pulled into her driveway and parked behind the house. When she stepped into her kitchen, Gooseberry wasn't at her ankles demanding whatever it was that he thought he needed at any particular moment — ear-scratching, a bowl of milk, a game of catnip mouse, more food in his dish — all the little things he assumed were rightfully his. Perhaps that was it. Perhaps the only thing wrong with her was the uncertain fate of her much loved feline.

With a whimsical refrigerator magnet, she attached a note for Uncle Miltie where he'd be sure to see it, near the freezer where the ice cream cartons resided. She glanced at her answering machine on the way out. No messages. Dave Wilkins would surely have called by now if there was fresh news.

As she came down the walk, Rocky, who had parked and was waiting for her, got out and opened the passenger-side door.

"Have you heard anything more about Frank Billingsly's dead sheep, or any of that?" She asked as she fastened her seatbelt.

Rocky adjusted his own seatbelt. "Nothing. I'm wondering if it's just been a combination of circumstances — incidents we've linked together in our minds. Where are we eating?"

"I thought you had some good place in mind."

"Nope. All places are alike to me. And that's a quote from . . . ?"

"Rudyard Kipling's *Just So Stories*, the 'Cat who Walked by Himself.' " Then a welter of emotions poured in on her. "It was one of my favorite books when I was a child." Gracie paused. Her voice broke. "Now, too, for that matter. And lovely Gooseberry is so much that cat, who walks in the wild alone." She rubbed her eyes.

Rocky studied her for the longest moment. "We'll eat later." He pulled away from the curb.

"But . . . ?" Gracie would have to admit that, on the whole, she hadn't felt that hungry. Still, she knew that taking the time to be with her friend over a meal would refresh her spirit as well as rest her tired body.

Then she saw where they were going: Rocky was taking her to the veterinarian's. She realized how true it was that sometimes friends know us better than we know ourselves. And she sent up a quick prayer that Gooseberry, when she saw him, would miraculously be on the mend.

"Rocky, thank you."

He parked right by the door and led her into the waiting room.

"May I help you?" There was a different receptionist on duty.

Gracie smiled. "I hope so. I'm Gooseberry's mother."

"I'll just go and check with the doctor." She returned swiftly. "This way, please."

Gracie knew the way, but she followed obediently.

Dave Wilkins popped out of a side room as they approached. She grinned. "Why, hello, Mrs. Parks! And Mr. Gravino." She looked at him. "I have those printouts for you. Stop by the desk on your way out and Annie will give them to you."

He nodded.

Dr. Wilkins waved an arm. "Just go on in. Annie, they know the way."

Rocky moved ahead enough to hold the door to the quiet room open. Gracie stepped inside. She paused for a moment of gratitude to God for providing her Gooseberry with this safe and peaceful haven.

"Gooseberry?" She opened the cage door and bent low to see him, settling herself in a comfortable crouch. "Gooseberry, dear."

She was almost too afraid to reach inside, so much did she fear what might be. She stretched just far enough to lay her hand in on that curved back. She could also feel that the fur was rough and dry. Normally, Gooseberry took such great pride in his fur. Gently, she stroked him.

Wait! Was he purring? No, not quite yet; but a weak sort of vibration was there, a feeble attempt.

And then, with his sandpaper tongue, he licked love across her hand.

25

With a grand flourish, Abe Wasserman set plates before Rocky and Gracie. "No contest, the best blintzes in Indiana! Enjoy!"

Gracie said, "Thank you, Abe."

He still stood there, watching Gracie with fond regard. "And the preliminary results of your professional analysis?"

"You know how I love them. More sour cream, please. I see Rocky's sneaking some of mine." Gracie looked up at Rocky. "I apologize again for coming apart like that at the vet's. I'm usually in much better control of myself."

"No apology necessary. It's been years since a woman cried on my shoulder. I actually liked it. Not that I don't hate to see you cry."

"Tears of joy aren't a bad thing."

He asked, "So what are you people going to do with that cocker spaniel once he gets out of the hospital? What's his name? Gent? He looks like he's going to recover."

Gracie nodded. "And Charlotte is looking so much better, too. I don't know. None of us has thought about it. He certainly shouldn't go to the pound. They get so many dogs, they have to destroy unclaimed animals.

"It's too bad Lester lives in an apartment with a No Pets policy. And that Don prefers cats. He's still nice enough, though, to have put signs around and to have placed an ad in your Lost and Found column. But, last I heard, there's been no response. He's such a sweet dog, we really should try a bit longer to find the owner."

"Since you three are paying the vet bill, and Dave's giving you a break on her fees, I'll help out with another bigger ad. Run a picture, too. That should get results."

"Oh, that's wonderful." Gracie knew she felt a whole lot better now. She really did.

For a moment, Rocky was silent. "So where did Paul and Dale take you yesterday?"

Gracie hesitated. Was this any of his business? The answer to that: As a newspaperman, he considered everything his business. Was there any harm in discussing it? Surely not. He and Paul shared the desire to bring Auto-Mate to town. She had to really think about where she'd been. It had been a whirlwind tour. "Frank's first, then that corner property on the Dorcester Pike, Morgans', the cow pasture on the east side next to the city limits, and Evanses'. Oh. And the Smith farm behind the Wal-Mart."

"Anything out by Coltrain?"

She frowned. "No. Isn't that area awfully hilly?"

"Yeah, kind of."

Then it became Gracie's turn to ask a question that had been on her mind. "Why haven't you mentioned anything in the paper about these mysterious illnesses, and the deaths?"

He shrugged. "I'm not sure it's real news. It could be unrelated events."

"And the stink bombs? They're certainly news."

"We wrote up the one at the police station."

"Two paragraphs all tucked away in the middle of the back section. And you never mentioned ours at Eternal Hope."

He shrugged again. "I should have, I know. In fact, I meant to. But the space went to something else when I wasn't paying attention." He changed the subject. "Are you going with Dale when she makes her presentation to the council?"

"I haven't decided yet."

Rocky's breast pocket played the opening bars of "The Star-Spangled Banner." "Sorry." He pulled his cell phone out and thumbed the button. He listened. "Yeah, Jess."

Gracie let her mind drift. Could she and Uncle Miltie possibly take in a dog? She couldn't see that. A whole parade of dogs had passed through her life during her marriage to El, and she was well aware of dogs' habits. The most dangerous of them was their predilection for lying down exactly where you are going to walk to next. Gracie could step over a cocker spaniel curled up in a doorway, but Uncle Miltie was very vulnerable to falling. She could not see taking the risk of deliberately harboring a dog that her uncle was likely to trip over.

Rocky pocketed his phone. "Sorry about that. Jess thinks the world is going to end. But then, he thinks that every time we get ready to go to press." He stood up. "I'll be back in a minute. I'll go settle up."

Through the door came sunshine on the hoof, laughing. It was one of the girls' sports teams, decked out in sweats in their school colors. As they crowded into the deli, one girl broke away and came over to Gracie, "Hi, Mrs. Parks!"

"Hello, Angie! Sit a moment, if you have time."

Angela Billingsly perched on the chair Rocky had just vacated. "I have to tell you how great that sauce was! Wow! I made it again last night, and it was delicious. Thanks!"

"You are so welcome. I'm glad it turned out well. How is everything going?"

"So far okay, I guess. Chuckie hasn't been around since Daddy chased him off. I guess that's okay. I try to stay away from him in the halls, but it isn't easy. The best part is, you can really see him coming. The hardest is chemistry class, because we're in the same period."

"Jeffrey Larson is younger than you by a year or two, though, isn't he? So he's in a different class?"

"No, he's in ours. They gave him special permission because he's such a science whiz. Chuckie's jealous of him. Says he's just as good a chemist as Jeffy, but Jeffy gets all the attention and nobody notices Chuckie. You know, in a way, he's right."

Rocky stepped up to the table. "Hello, Angela."

"Hi, Mr. Gravino." Angie stood up. "I better go. They'll all have their stuff and I didn't order yet. 'Bye."

Angie seemed so much more chipper than she had a few days ago. Was it simply that she was in the presence of her exuberant teammates, or was she really that glad to be rid of Chuckie?

Rocky was off to his office to settle a crisis, so Gracie offered to walk home. But he was having none of it. They talked of Gooseberry's recovery as he drove her home. Halfway up the walk, Gracie by chance happened to glance down the street.

Near the corner a little car was parked. And she could just barely make out the driver's green hair.

26

Gracie sat in the subdued light of her living room, surrounded by reminders of El and her son Arlen's childhood and school years. She realized she hadn't talked to him since Gooseberry's medical emergency. And now, when she did, would she want to fill him in on her current worry?

Why was Chuckie Moon spying on her?

Not to mention: What was going on out at Frank Billingsly's? Who threw the stink bombs? And why was Rocky downplaying this so much? Normally, the *Mason County Gazette* made sure it covered local news down to the last Little League home run and the town's newest litter of puppies.

And, while on that subject, what could they do about Gent the cocker spaniel?

Plus, why had Pastor Paul dragged her into this factory mess? It was a role she didn't wish to play. And wasn't there some way to allow progress without destroying so much? Channelization. She shuddered.

Finally, Gracie still smarted from The Potato Salad That Tastes Like a Banana incident. Uncle Miltie had sworn he hadn't done it. If he wasn't responsible, who was? No one else that she knew of could have stirred it once it left her house.

She hated it when so much descended on her all at once. And the biggest question of all was what, if anything, was she going to do? She wasn't one to sit quietly by, hoping that it all somehow would conveniently go away. Besides, problems almost never did that. They festered. They grew. They haunted. That's why they were problems. And they almost always left behind fallout.

The phone rang, startling her from her reverie.

With a sigh, she set down her tea. "Hello?"

"This is Dr. Wilkins, Mrs. Parks. How are you doing?"

"How is Gooseberry?"

"He's doing better all the time, but I'd like to keep him another day or two."

"Of course. I'm so close it's easy to visit to cheer on his recovery."

"Actually, I'm calling more about the cocker. He's been responding well, and he's ready to be released. My receptionist called Mr. Delano and he asked her to call Mr.

Twomley. So she called Mr. Twomley and he asked her to call you. Anyway, I told her I'd call you. Apparently you are the dog enthusiast."

"No, I'm the fall-back position. But I'll be happy to take him for now. I'll come by in about an hour. Is that satisfactory?"

"Fine." She added, "I threw in a rabies shot, since we've no way of knowing if he was vaccinated. If you don't find the owner, you'll want to set up the parvo series for him."

"Thank you. Just put the rabies tag on a collar. I'll get him a collar and leash."

Gracie pondered things a moment, then called Rocky at the paper.

"How quickly can we place the bigger ad for the cocker spaniel? I just heard from the animal hospital. He's ready to leave."

"Where will you keep him until you find him a home?"

"Here, I suppose. I'll set him up in the garage so he doesn't get underfoot and cause Uncle Miltie to take a tumble. I'm worried about that. That's why I'd like to find him a place as soon as possible." She waited a polite length of time while she listened to silence on the other end. Then she asked, "Rocky?"

"I'm thinking. Okay, here's what you do.

Put him on a leash and walk him up Hollister to McCall."

"Yes, but . . ."

"I'll meet you somewhere around the corner of McCall and Fifth. What would that be? About an hour?"

"Yes, but . . ."

"Good. See you there." And he hung up.

She sighed. Were men this cagey on purpose? If there was a plan, she'd prefer knowing it. Still, experience had taught her to trust her friend the editor. Rocky was gruff, sometimes, but always good-hearted.

It took nearly half an hour for her to walk over to the veterinarian's office and complete the paperwork. She remembered back when you could take your dog or cat in for a shot or procedure and then gave the vet several dollars in cash. That's all. Not so much as a receipt. Those days, she reflected, were gone forever.

The vet's assistant had chosen an elegant little leather collar, appropriate for a cocker deserving the name Gent. As she approached his cage, the dog seemed to recognize Gracie immediately and wagged his tail. She slipped the collar on him, making sure to praise him as she did.

"He's been in the run outside yesterday and this morning and seems to be all right as stamina goes. But I wouldn't make him walk too far."

Gracie snapped the leash she'd been given on the ring. It was certainly a pretty dog, although his fur was patchy, with big chunks gone from the outer coat. "Taking those burs out must have been quite a chore."

"Oh my, yes. And he was so patient about it. He knew what we were doing. We didn't even have to sedate him. Gent has very good manners." The girl gave him a final affectionate rub around the ears. "Let us know where he ends up, would you?"

"Certainly." Gracie stood up then and led her temporary charge out into the waiting room.

From behind her, the girl called, "Look out."

"What?" Gracie turned toward the desk.

The girl grinned. "He grows on you. Good luck."

Gracie continued out into the afternoon sun.

Now what? As Gent busied himself examining grass tufts and liner stones beside the parking lot, Gracie tried to figure out what next. For want of any better ideas, she started up the street toward Hollister.

When she sat for a moment on a bus-stop bench, Gent gratefully flopped down beside her. They both rested, equally uncertain as to what the end of all this would be. Gent, however, wasn't looking so anxious.

A block this side of McCall, she saw a familiar figure turn the corner up ahead, walking in this direction. Here came Rocky, with his basset, Rover, on a leash!

If anyone had asked Gracie whether God has a sense of humor, one possible answer might be, "Watch a basset walk." Rover's knobby little legs trotted rapidly, as he cruised along a few inches off the cement. His huge ears flopped, so that, with every choppy little stride, he came very close to stepping on them. Suddenly and occasionally, he would make a ninety-degree turn to investigate the base of a fence post or bush.

Gracie understood that the basset and Rocky had walked many a mile together. They kept pace with each other comfortably, despite the dog's tendency to side excursions.

Halfway up the block, the two animals met. Gracie braced herself for quick action in case one or both of them decided the other needed to be dispatched immediately. But they did not. Amid embarrassingly intimate sniffing and tail-wagging, they accepted each other with a high approval rating.

Rocky pointed, "Let's go down here. You know that nice little park about a block from here? It's not very big, but we can let them run a little."

"I think mine will prefer to sleep. He's still recovering and seems to tire easily." They began a stroll made all the more casual by the two dogs' constant sidetracks and explorations. "Now what's going on here?"

"Well, from your tone of voice on the phone, I didn't detect you jumping up and down at the chance to have a dog. Now on the other hand, I'm already set up for dogs. Doggy door, fenced yard, the whole nine yards. So I figured if someone has to keep the mutt until we find him a home, it might as well be me." Rocky looked at her. "Logical?"

"Beautiful. It's extremely thoughtful of you."

In fact, the more she thought about it, the better it sounded. What a fine solution to Gent's homeless condition!

And what did the dogs think of the idea? So far, they seemed to accept one another. While Rocky and Gracie sat on a bench and discussed the weather, Gent and —

"Rocky, why Rover? He doesn't *look* like a Rover."

"Well, how many dogs do you know actually named Rover? People avoid it because they think it's too common, but, in fact, it's almost never used."

The dogs were exploring together, sharing their discoveries. Gent watered the swing set and teeter-totter. Then Rover ambled off on wider explorations, his ears dragging, and Gent curled up at Gracie's feet.

Gracie explained to her friend the details of Gent's discovery and recovery. And by the time they reached Rocky's house, Gent and Rover appeared to be lifelong friends. They trotted right inside without incident. Rover had accepted the newcomer as a brother — or, at least, a cousin.

They had obviously ignored the lack of family resemblance.

27

"Hello there!" Roy Bell augmented his cheery greeting by knocking. The balding leprechaun's wizened face peered in at Gracie through the mesh of the kitchen screen door.

Gracie stood up from the table. "Good morning. What brings you?" She swung the door open wide. "Come in."

"I was in the neighborhood, so I figured I'd stop by." He stood in the doorway, looking anxiously about. "That cat isn't hanging around here just now, is it?"

"No. It's safe to enter. Coffee?" Gracie went after a mug for Roy and hers for herself.

He leaned back, as the chair creaked in response. "Remember some time back, you asked me to look at your foundation? You said no hurry, just when I had time."

"I remember." Gracie also felt that the exchange seemed to have taken place at least a year and a half ago.

"Well, a project cancelled on me and I have a couple days, so I thought I might get on that. I took another look at it as I was coming in. I'd guess two days, less than five hundred dollars."

Gracie's eyebrows rose. "That's a very good offer, Roy. I was anticipating that it would be considerably more." She poured for the two of them.

"Nope. All we have to do is run some reinforcing rods down there, mortar the loose stuff and point the blocks. I'll just hire on some temporary help and have it done in no time."

"That would be good. I don't want it to deteriorate much further. After all, it is the foundation." Gracie put the last of a batch of anise cookies out on a dessert plate and sat down.

With exquisite care, Roy chose one of the dozen identical cookies on the dish. "Say, uh, I hear you were out with that factory rep looking at sites."

Oh, no. Already, Gracie didn't like the way this was going. "As I understand it, no one has made any decisions. It's all up in the air yet."

"I heard all kinds of things. Just wondered where the truth lay."

"Roy? Why are you and Harry so adamantly opposed to this factory? I understand that Harry could be afraid, somehow, it could be competition, but why are you?"

"We have such a pretty little town here, with some unspoiled country around it. There's nowhere prettier than Mason County, and you know I'm right. Rotten shame to see the outskirts turn into more suburbs with a factory and everything."

"I certainly can't argue with that."

"Now over around Coltrain, in those uplands, that wouldn't be so bad. Down here, this is prime farm country, and it's not just about scenic beauty. When you pave it over, you're paving over tomorrow's dinner. But out around there, it wouldn't have such an impact. Know what I mean?"

Gracie nodded. "You're probably right."

"Better believe I'm right! Not only that, the folks over around Coltrain want it. I mean they all really want it. It isn't like here, where some's for and most are against." He snatched another cookie and stood up. "If I start your work this afternoon, I can have it done in two days, before my next one's needing me."

"I'd like your offer in writing before you begin, please."

"Of course. I'll drop it by later on. Better get going." He paused by the kitchen door.

"And if I don't get it done as quick as I thought, there's Sunday. I can come in on Sunday and finish it up. A cushion, you know?"

"You mean work over Sunday?"

"Sure. One day or another, makes no difference to me."

And that casual comment, a throwaway line actually, made Gracie feel very sad.

"Yep," Roy said, "over around Coltrain, now there would be the perfect place for a factory like they're talking about."

He just about ran over Marge leaving, or, closer to the truth, he was nearly run over by Marge. They greeted each other warily, and Marge proceeded into Gracie's kitchen in an excited rush.

"Charlotte's home! They let me bring her home this morning!" Her curls, normally tightly arranged in the manner of an exotic bird, now stuck out from her head at odd angles. She was obviously less concerned with what she'd seen in the mirror than she was with Charlotte's happy return. Vanity took a back seat to her warm heart when the little dog was concerned.

Gracie hugged her friend exuberantly and danced her about the room. She then ushered Marge to a chair. "That's wonderful! There's a little coffee left, or I can make fresh."

"Both!" Marge replied. "And let's have some cinnamon toast, too, with lots of butter."

"I haven't gotten a chance to tell you the latest about that sick cocker that Don and Lester and I found. He —"

But she stopped because Marge was obviously bursting to narrate all over again every single detail of Charlotte's ordeal, right down to the parts that Gracie already knew.

Why interfere with Marge's happiness, she thought. Talking in overdrive was Marge's way of expressing extremes. How long she might have gone on was anyone's guess. She was finally interrupted, though, by the front doorbell, just as she was finishing her third piece of toast.

She frowned. "Expecting someone?"

"No, but that never stops them from showing up." Gracie went out to answer the door because Uncle Miltie was at the senior center, she knew, with his pinochle pals.

Pastor Paul, his bike helmet tucked under his arm, stood on the front porch.

"Come in!"

"I didn't know if you would be home, but since I was riding by . . ."

"Marge is in the kitchen. We were just celebrating her Charlotte's return from the pet hospital. Please join us."

"There are far lesser things to celebrate. I'd love to." He followed her to the back of the house.

"Marge?" Gracie studied her kitchen table. The plate that once held cinnamon toast lay empty but for a few buttery crumbs. "I don't have any more bread. Is there any at your house?"

"Sure — I'll be right back!"

Pastor Paul cleared his throat. "The reason I came over — I'm not sure how to explain this."

"I'm patient. Just try."

"I'm thinking of resigning. Giving up my position at Eternal Hope."

She barely managed a surprised "Why?"

"I'm just not cut out for this." He spread his hands. "Remember a couple days ago, when we went out with Dale?" He watched her nod. "I said you didn't seem to fear anything and you mentioned how you'd felt when your husband died. You didn't describe those fears in detail. You just assumed it was common ground and that I understood. But I didn't, Gracie. And I don't. I haven't the slightest idea what you went through because I myself have never had that kind of basic life experience."

"And, therefore, you should quit? I don't understand."

"Basic life experience, Gracie. Almost everyone I can think of at Eternal Hope has had more of it than I have. They've — you've — been through more. You *know* more. You're wiser. I'm just a kid. How can I hope to counsel people, even comfort them in the best way?"

"Paul." She looked him in the eye. "I hear your distress, hear what you're telling me. But I have no idea what to say or do. Therefore I'm not going to say or do anything. Let me think about it, will you? I cannot advise you immediately. I simply must think about it."

"Fair enough. I'm not sure why I came. But I know I trust you. I can certainly wait awhile before acting on this. But I do plan to act on it, unless you can come up with some awfully good reasons why not."

"You must listen to your own heart, of course. But, most importantly, to God. It's not at all a bad time to pray. Will you promise me you'll try that?"

"Yes, of course," he replied. "Thank you, Gracie."

Now what? The doorbell had sounded again. She excused herself and headed back to the door.

There stood Jessica Larson. "Hello, Gracie. May I come in?"

"Certainly." Gracie stepped aside.

Even as she headed toward the kitchen, she began to speak. "Gracie, I need you. You've got to help me."

28

There sat Pastor Paul in the kitchen, greatly troubled. Marge could be heard coming in the back door. Now here stood a woman she didn't respect much, begging her for help.

Why me? Gracie cried out silently to God.

And God quietly returned with, *Why not you?*

Frankly, she hadn't a good answer. "Pastor Paul and Marge are in the kitchen making more cinnamon toast. It's great comfort food. Won't you join us?"

"Oh, no. I'll just come back later." Jessica hesitated.

Gracie waited.

Suddenly her new visitor changed her mind. "Oh, why not?"

In the kitchen, Marge was mixing more cinnamon and sugar. She beamed. "Why, hello, Jessica! You're just in time."

Moments later, they were all sitting around the table, messily enjoying the familiar blend of tastes and textures.

"As I said, the reason I came by," Jessica began, "was to ask your help, Gracie." She licked her fingers daintily.

"In what way?"

"Charles Moon." She addressed not just Gracie but everyone there, looking from face to face. "He is one of the students in Jeffrey's chemistry class, and he's causing a serious problem. He has threatened Jeffrey."

"As in 'physically'?" Marge was aghast.

"Yes. Physical violence. He says he's going to make Jeffrey sorry if he gets an A in his chemistry class." She emended her statement. "If Jeffrey gets an A, I mean." She went on, explaining, "Jeffrey is younger than anyone else in his chem class. And now he's so worried about Charles, he's afraid to go to school."

This was the first time Gracie could ever remember that Jessica Larson was anything but in total control. Now she was faced with a volatile situation that threatened to affect the physical safety of her only child.

A pang of sympathy seized Gracie. "Did you talk to Bud Smith?"

"Of course. I went to the principal first. He said that he could call Charles in and talk to him, but he didn't think it would do much good. And once the —" She fished for words a moment — "the deed is done, it's too late. My son is in the hospital or worse and Charles is suspended. I don't know what to do. I just don't!"

As she worriedly nibbled at her toast, Gracie tried to think of some way to help. But if she could not control Chuckie in her own life, how could she hope to control him in someone else's?

Gracie glanced at Marge. Marge appeared just as perplexed. Only Pastor Paul looked serene. "Gracie? Did you recycle your phone book yet?"

"It's out in the garage."

"May I have it?"

"I'll get you the current one."

"No, I'd like the old one, please."

What could she say? She went out to the garage. A minute or two of rummaging about in the bin produced the old directory. She brought it in and gave it to Pastor Paul.

He stood up as she handed it to him. "Thank you, Gracie. Your cinnamon toast gets my highest recommendation. And now if you will excuse me, ladies." He retrieved his helmet from under his chair. Gracie saw him to the door.

Jessica was frowning. "While you were out in the garage, he said he has reason to think that Charles won't be a problem anymore. Don't I wish it were true!" She peered at Gracie. "Why did he come by, anyway?"

Gracie looked at her innocently. "Pastoral visit, I suppose."

"In bike shorts?"

Jessica remained a half an hour longer, seemingly reluctant to forego the security of Gracie's kitchen.

Marge gathered the dishes after she'd left. "I feel sorry for her. Her son is facing a serious problem. But I can't help but say she really gets on my nerves, anyway."

"I feel about the same," Gracie agreed. "I don't think that we can —"

The phone interrupted her. She answered it.

"This is Bud Smith, Gracie. Good afternoon."

"Good afternoon, Bud!" Gracie raised a finger, a "wait a minute" gesture to Marge. "What can I do for you?"

"I'm hosting a get-together for my teachers next week. Can you cater it for me?"

"Next week is fairly short notice, but I'm sure I can do it." Gracie wagged her hand toward the notepad and pencil on the counter. "What are the details?"

Marge fetched the paper and pencil, watching her.

"How about," he asked, "stopping by the school? We can discuss it."

"I'll come over this afternoon." Gracie thanked him and thumbed the hang-up button. "The high school principal wants me to cater next week. Can you help?"

"Goody!" Marge rubbed her hands together. "If we do a good job with it, other teachers will ask you. I have to get home now. I'm minding the store this evening."

"And I'll get the information we need this afternoon."

Thus it was that Gracie found herself at the high school as it was about to let out. When she arrived, the students were in the halls, slamming locker doors, yelling and laughing.

She checked in at the office, the standard procedure for visitors, and was surprised to see *Paul Meyer* signed into the book just ahead of her.

"I'd like to see Mr. Smith," she announced.

"He's out in the parking lot, I think. He took some stuff to his car."

"I'll look for him out there." Gracie hurried down the hall and out the side door to the parking area.

And stopped cold. Chuckie was crossing her path thirty feet in front of her. He was headed for his car, she was certain. And there was Pastor Paul approaching Chuckie from the other side.

They were too far away for Gracie to hear any words. She could only see the body language. Pastor Paul, all smiles, shook hands, obviously introducing himself. Then he displayed Gracie's old phone book. He was saying something that made Chuckie smirk.

Pastor Paul gripped the phone book with both hands and then, casually, ripped it in two. Widthwise.

Gracie was so enthralled she almost forgot to watch Chuckie's reaction. The green-haired lad looked appropriately startled — and respectful. Curious, even, Gracie thought.

Then Paul laid a long, strong arm across Chuckie's shoulders, half a phone book still in hand. Chuckie flinched. Still talking, the pastor gave Chuckie a few smart pats on the back and walked away. Chuckie called after him, and Paul returned, just for a minute or so more.

Bud Smith stepped in beside her, a few seconds too late to witness the encounter. "Good afternoon, Gracie! Come on inside."

"Thanks for thinking of me." And Gracie followed him into the building. As she stepped through the door she glanced back at Chuckie Moon. The boy still stood beside his car, looking off to where Paul Meyer was biking out of the high school parking lot.

29

Frank Billingsly was handing Gracie a cardboard carton. "Same order next week?"

"Yes, thank you, Frank! How's Angie doing?" Gracie's question was really, *Is Chuckie still a problem?* but, of course, she didn't phrase it that way.

But Frank answered the question she was really asking. "She's doing fine, it seems. Haven't had a C. Moon problem since that day you were by. I'm hoping it's all blown over by now."

They were standing out by the curb, leaning on his truck and enjoying the morning sun. The weather folk on Uncle Miltie's loud morning news were promising rain by close of day. Gracie wanted to enjoy the sun while she could.

"Frank? Is your creek much given to flooding?"

"Like you wouldn't believe. It would worry Noah! But not often, mind you. Maybe once a year, on the average. Less.

Oh, sure, it runs high every now and then. All creeks do. I don't mean that. But when it really goes, it goes. I've seen it rise eight feet in two hours, if the rains upstream are right. It'll just about fill up that sheep pasture."

And the creek bank from the usual water level to the meadow was, at most, three feet. Gracie could just picture why developers might want to channelize the stream.

Now here came Roy Bell's rattletrap truck down the street. With a cheery wave, he pulled into Gracie's driveway and parked by the corner of the house.

Frank reached for the door handle. "Got lots of eggs to deliver yet this morning. Take care, Gracie."

"Blessings, Frank." Gracie stepped back as the pickup pulled away.

Gracie walked back to where Roy had dropped his tailgate. Now he was getting out tools and rebar.

"Got a kid coming over this afternoon to help. I can have a lot of it done by the time it rains tonight."

"Isn't rain a problem?"

"Not with cement. Helps, with cement."

"Mm." She watched for a moment more. "I'll be in the house. If you need anything, just holler."

"I will." And he set to work.

The television set in the kitchen was still blaring as Gracie stepped inside. Uncle Miltie was alternating his attention between his oatmeal and the late morning news. He was now absorbed in the commuter traffic report, despite the fact that he did not drive.

Gracie continued into the living room. She really ought to clean the house today. She would start upstairs and —

The phone rang. Gracie was certain that if God is just, there would be no phones in heaven. "Hello?"

"Hello, Mrs. Parks? This is Dale Springer."

Here was still another complication that Gracie hoped would be banished from heaven — commitments she did not volunteer for. "What can I do for you?"

"I was wondering if you ever do baby-sitting. Paul Meyer said that you sometimes take on short-term projects, so to speak. It would only be for the next two days or so." She hesitated. When Gracie's reply was not immediately forthcoming, she added, "I pay well."

"I'm sure you do, but I'm afraid I'm tied up with other pursuits. Thank you for the offer, though."

"I'm at my wit's end. Two sitters have fallen through on me now. I'm not here in

Mason County much longer, but I have a lot left to do until I go back."

"This is for Roger, I assume."

"Yes. He'll go back to school when we get home. But I couldn't leave him there and come here for two weeks. Today he's at loose ends and still not old enough to be on his own."

Just then Gracie had a brilliant idea. "Have you tried Jessica Larson, Jeffrey's mother? She's at home most days, and Jeffrey and Roger seem to get along."

"Mm." The voice at the other end paused. "I could try there. Thank you."

"You're welcome." Gracie hung up and headed upstairs. While she was doing the bedrooms, she might as well change the beds. She paused at the hall closet for the sheets.

The phone rang. Gracie sighed and answered.

"This is Dale Springer again. Mrs. Parks, could you please help me just for now and take Roger until school gets out this afternoon? Mrs. Larson has a dental appointment, but she intends to be back by the time Jeffrey gets home. That was a good idea of yours. Really, it was."

"I'm not sure." Gracie sat down on the edge of her stripped bed to think. Did she really want to do this? No, she certainly did not. Ought she to do this? That was another story. When people needed help, you helped them when they needed it, not at your convenience. With a heavy heart, she said, "Yes, I think I can."

"That's wonderful! You know where we're staying."

"No, but a quick guess would be Cordelia Fountain's."

"Very good. Yes. Roger will be in the parlor. I have to run. I'm already late. Thank you so much, Mrs. Parks!"

Click.

Gracie stared at her phone. Why did she let herself get into these things? She'd just have to bring Roger over here and let him help her clean. Maybe he could pitch in to get lunch ready, too. She would feed him and make sure he arrived at the Larsons' when Jeffrey did.

"Uncle Miltie?" She called out. "I'm running over to Main Street! Be back shortly!" If he heard her at all, he paid no attention.

Roy moved his truck cheerfully, waving to Gracie as she backed out onto the street.

A few high cirrus clouds were starting to turn the blue sky milky. Usually, cirrus preceded rain by at least twenty-four hours. Maybe it would even hold off until Roy finished the foundation work. She pulled into the driveway of Mrs. Fountain's tourist home.

Cordelia herself was seated at the small writing desk in the front parlor. She was going through receipts, making entries in a twelve-column ledger. "Ah! There you are. I was beginning to worry." She came over to Gracie, and told her, "I do not do baby-sitting, and that's that. Roger? Here's Mrs. Parks."

From a huge settee in the parlor, Roger Springer scrambled to his feet.

Gracie smiled at Mrs. Fountain. "Thanks for looking after him until I got here. Mrs. Springer and I both appreciate it." She hesitated. "Don't you use a spread sheet — you know, a computer program — for your records?"

"I tried it and the disk crashed." Cordelia raised her pencil defiantly. "When this crashes, I just run it through the pencil sharpener, and nothing's lost."

Laughing, Gracie took her leave. She walked out and down the front steps with Roger beside her.

"What grade are you in at school?" Gracie pulled out onto the street.

"Sixth."

Silence.

"How old are you?"

"Twelve."

Silence.

Gracie thought for a moment about the day she walked out across Frank's sheep pasture. "Didn't I see you out on a bike a couple days ago?"

"Yeah, maybe."

"If your mom and you are only in town for a couple of weeks, where did you get the bike? Bring it along?"

"Borrowed it."

Long silence.

"I don't have much at my house in the way of toys or books. Shall we stop at the library on the way home?"

"I don't have a card."

"Not a problem. I do."

She took his silence as a yes and detoured down Oak Street. They were early and had to wait five minutes on the front step until the doors opened.

The boy would never be an athlete, but he was surely a promising bookworm. He went directly to the science fiction section and began scanning the shelves. Gracie herself skimmed the cookbooks, glanced over the travel books and gave the new acquisitions shelf a hard look. No mysteries she hadn't already read.

Eventually she selected a coffee-table book on China and a memoir of Amish life. Roger was also successful, emerging with a small pile of his own. They checked out their treasures and climbed back into the car.

Gracie glanced at the books on Roger's lap as she eased into traffic. "I could never develop much interest in sci-fi. I tried a couple times."

"Ever read Tolkien? *The Hobbit*?"

"Oh, my, yes! Devoured the trilogy."

"That's all sci-fi. Actually, it's fantasy, but fantasy and science fiction are usually lumped together. Most books are a little of both. Most of the good ones anyway."

"I never thought about it, but you're right. Owning a powerful ring that makes you invisible is like science fiction. What about Anne McCaffrey's white dragons?"

"I read those when I was seven."

"Who's your favorite author now?"

"Ray Bradbury."

"I know some of his short stories," Gracie told him. "Myself, I like mysteries." They finished the ride home in companionable silence.

Uncle Miltie was gone, the TV set in the kitchen silent. That was a relief. Except for the occasional loud clunk outside where

Roy was working, the house was fairly quiet.

This was going much better than she had hoped. She asked, "Do you have to have a strong science background to enjoy the kind of sci-fi that isn't fantasy?"

"Not to read it, although it helps. You need a lot of science if you're going to write it." He hesitated only a moment before adding, "I want to write it. Professionally, I mean. So I'm taking lots of science in school."

"Like Jeffrey."

"Naw, not like Jeffrey. All he cares about is looking good so his mom doesn't yell at him as much. He doesn't care if he actually learns anything or not. Like, he had that remote control helicopter but he couldn't get it to work right. So I showed him how to get more power out of his fuel and how to program it right. And it worked."

"I was there when he flew it into the living room."

"I like working on learning the hard stuff. You know, really learning it, like quantum physics. You have to really *know* the stuff, not just get good grades. Hey, can I help you with anything?"

"Well, I was going to clean the house."

"Great! I never get to clean at home. We have a cleaning lady. I'm real good at bathrooms."

Will wonders never cease? Gracie had just been handed not a lemon but the lemonade itself. She took advantage of it.

Roger ended up staying for supper and not going to the Larsons after all. They called his mother and made the arrangement. Gracie dropped him off at Cordelia's on her way to choir practice.

The practice went as practices always did — sporadically, as one section, then another, struggled to get their parts right. When it was over, Gracie took her music down to the vestry and retrieved her purse. It had been a long day. Roger Springer had turned out to be a charming boy, friendly and knowledgeable once he warmed up. But he'd worn her out, nonetheless.

Lester, Rick and Don were gathered beside Don's van. Gracie had every intention of getting in her own car, driving home and taking a warm bath. Instead, she found herself walking toward them.

Don was holding what looked like a fistful of reports. ". . . Mostly particulates. Standard water stuff. But this one here, where you fell in, Lester, some pretty heavy hydrocarbons here. Also downstream a little way."

Lester craned his neck to see. "That's not just antifreeze. Or am I wrong?"

Don looked grim. "Folks, the bottom line is, if this stuff ever gets into the public water supply, we've got a very serious problem."

30

Rocky's car had a sunroof, and today not one dog's head was sticking out of it but two. Rover's basset ears threatened to take him aloft if the speed topped thirty. And Gent's cocker spaniel ears were very nearly as aerodynamic. Gracie was standing out front watching Uncle Miltie, her ace shrub-pruner, clipping some untidy branches.

The moment Rocky stopped, the heads disappeared inside. He got out and pointed sternly at the happy animals. "Stay! That means you!"

He joined Gracie. "Good morning. And good morning to you, Miltie," he called.

"It certainly is a good morning! The vet's office just called. I'm just going now to get Gooseberry and bring him home where he belongs."

"It's been a long haul."

"Indeed it has."

"I was wondering if you'd heard anything

about Dale Springer looking at property over around Coltrain."

"Sort of. Why?"

"My engine's warmed up. Why don't I just take you over to the vet now with me?" She noticed he hadn't answered her.

"Transporting a temperamental cat in a carful of dogs doesn't lend itself well. Thanks, but —"

"Oh, don't worry about them." He marched to his passenger side and opened the door. "You and you. Into the back seat!" He stepped aside. "There you go."

"Gent certainly responds well."

"We're old friends already, but he knows who's boss."

Secretly, she was glad he'd offered to accompany her. Now she could hold the cat carrier on her lap.

Rocky chose this moment to return to the previous topic. "The reason I asked: I got a letter to the editor this morning. It rolled on and on about how this part of the county, with its farms, doesn't need a factory but the Coltrain area could more easily support one. I was hoping you could shed some light here, having gone around with Paul Meyer and Dale Springer."

"Who signed the letter?"

"Name Withheld. He sends us lots of

mail. He's almost as prolific a writer as Ann Onymous."

"You're sure it's a he?"

"Pretty sure."

Roy Bell. But should she say so? "Incidentally," — this was one comment she could make safely — "I didn't see the ad for Gent yet."

"Yeah, well, we haven't had room. I'll get to it. As long as he's got a place to stay, there's no rush. Right?"

"Right."

At All Creatures, after she'd settled the bill, Gracie suddenly heard a commotion of some sort at the back of the building. And then the vet's assistant appeared empty-handed. "There seems to have been a mix-up, Mrs. Parks. Your cat isn't ready yet. We'll have to call you about when you can come get him."

"But I just paid and everything."

"I'm sorry. It's just not possible right now. *Please.*"

Rocky looked at Gracie. "Let's go see what's going on here. Where's Dave Wilkins?"

The young woman stepped into the hall entryway, making a human roadblock. "I said I'm very sorry, but you can't —"

Too late. They could, and he did. Gracie

followed Rocky down the hall, like a row-boat behind an icebreaker. They marched directly to the quiet room.

Gooseberry's cage door hung ajar. Anxiously, Gracie ran to it and peered in. It was empty.

She wheeled to Rocky. Her distress was barely containable. "Where is he? What's happening?"

Her champion turned on the receptionist and roared, "Where's Dr. Wilkins?"

"With another patient. I can't — you can't —"

"Dave!" Rocky shouted, and Gracie was so glad to be in the company of someone so accustomed to getting his own way.

"Hey, Dave!" he bellowed again.

"In here!" came a muted voice.

Rocky strode halfway down the side hall and opened a door.

It was the operating room; Gracie recognized it immediately. Dr. Wilkins, in mask and rubber gloves, was working on a cat tied down to the table. With a rush of relief, Gracie saw instantly that its fur was not orange.

"Hello, Rocky. Annie, what's going on here?"

From behind Gracie, the young woman stammered, "They wouldn't stay out front! I told them to — I couldn't . . ."

"Gracie's cat is gone." Rocky was succinct in his reporting of the situation.

"Not in the carrying crate?" The doctor looked at Annie.

"I put him in it and cleaned the cage to make it ready for this one like you said and now he's gone!"

Demanded Gracie, "When did you last see him?"

"When I set his crate by the door. But he — but you — I don't — gosh, where could he be? This is terrible!"

"Search the place," Rocky ordered.

"I'll be done here in fifteen minutes." Dr. Wilkins went back to her work.

Gracie closed the door gently behind her. She stood in the hall a moment to think it through. The girl had taken Gooseberry out of his cage and put him in his travel box. She had set the box then by a door. When she'd returned for him he was gone, and she'd tried her best to cover. Where would Gooseberry go?

Could he get out of the building? Not out front, not without being noticed. Not out the back door; it led only to the fenced dog runs. She looked around the corner of the hall to the side door, the one with the porch light over it. It stood wide open, sunlight streaming in.

At the far end of the hall, another girl, her back to Gracie, was whistling as she mopped the floor.

Gracie called, "Young lady! Did you see a big orange cat?"

She stopped to look at Gracie. "You mean Gooseberry?" She set the mop against the wall. "I had to prep the O.R. last evening so I didn't have time to clean. That's why I'm here this morning. But I haven't seen your cat. I'm sorry."

Gracie nodded. "Thanks!" She ran back up the hall. With Rocky she searched every room, including the storeroom. And Gracie whispered her cat's name into every corner, every crevice.

An hour later, totally defeated, Rocky said, "I'll take you home."

Gracie replied sadly, "I suppose you might as well."

She rode back to her house with the empty travel box in her lap.

Roy was digging around her foundation when they pulled up. But he stood up to greet her, scowling. "You were supposed to keep that bloody cat away from me!"

"What . . . ?"

"How am I supposed to get anything done when your crazy animal is prowling around making me even crazier?"

"What . . . ?"

"If it wasn't your cat, Gracie, I swear I'd have clubbed him with a shovel! He's inside now. So let's keep him there, okay? You won't get me back in that house for love nor money!"

"What . . . ?"

Gracie reached the back steps ahead of Rocky. At the table sat Uncle Miltie, eating a meatloaf sandwich. The TV set was blaring.

Uncle Miltie said, "Hi."

Rocky said, "Well, I'll be."

From his accustomed place atop the back of the chair by the kitchen door, Gooseberry greeted her, "Meow."

31

When the Eternal Hope choir sang of sin and death, grief seized its listeners. When the choir sang of holy retribution, the congregation trembled. And when the choir sang of God's redemption, the rafters rang for joy.

Today the rafters rang. The anthem as performed in the worship service went so much better than it had in rehearsal. Gracie sustained her high note, a B flat, as all around her, sopranos and tenors sang counterpoint. And then Amy Cantrell's clear soprano climbed out on top of everyone else with the final paean to God's eternal majesty.

Slowly, Barb lowered her arms. The choir director was obviously having a difficult time trying to contain her pride and happiness.

"At least it went well today, on Sunday," Marge whispered to Gracie as she jammed her music into her folder.

Gracie tried to pay attention to Pastor

Paul's message, but it was hard. She kept seeing him in bike shorts at her kitchen table, expressing his fears and doubts. It seemed so strange: He was a powerful speaker! Just listen to him.

Finally the choir stood to complete the service and sing the recessional. Gracie took her music down to the vestry. "That was beautiful, Amy. You just get better and better."

Amy blushed. "Thanks, Gracie. It went well this morning, didn't it?" She put her music sleeve on the shelf.

"Gracie?" Rick Harding handed her a sheaf of papers. "This was everything I could find on the Web that's pertinent to the kind of toxic effect you describe. It isn't much. There's a lot of stuff out there, but, unfortunately, none of it seems to apply directly. Your best bet is still antifreeze, or a related glycol."

"Thanks for all your effort, Rick."

"Oh, that reminds me." Amy paused in the doorway. "I was going to ask a friend of mine who's an herbalist, remember? She says she doesn't know of any that would do that, at least not that quickly. She says you'll have to go into chemical analysis, and she's betting it will have something to do with anthrax."

"Anthrax?"

Amy shrugged. "That's what she says. But she's an aromatherapist now. Bye!"

"Good-bye." Anthrax! Willow Bend was hardly the setting for some movie-of-the-week-type thriller!

It was raining now. Gracie took her time walking out to her car. She didn't mind getting wet, and, besides, wasn't it good for the complexion?

Then she glimpsed Uncle Miltie coming out of the church, so she pulled out and drove around to pick him up.

Once settled, he quizzed his niece, "Where're we going to eat?"

"I thought we'd just go home. Leftovers."

"Hmph. That's the trouble with living with a cook. You never get to eat out."

"If you *weren't* living with a cook, where would you like to go?"

"Out. I don't care. Anywhere."

"Abe's deli, Sunday brunch?"

"Sure."

There'd be a table available in twenty minutes, the waitress told them.

"We'll wait," Uncle Miltie replied.

But they didn't have to. Don Delano was waving them over to where he was seated with Lester.

The two men politely stood up as she approached. Don helped Uncle Miltie get

231

comfortable and then seated Gracie with a flourish.

They ordered a basket of fresh onion rolls, followed by a platter of smoked fish, then scrambled eggs with salami and crispy hash-browns.

Uncle Miltie was not one to miss the opportunity to tell one of his jokes to an audience. He started, "There were two golfers. The first one says, 'I have the greatest ball in the world, you can't lose it.'

"The second one says, 'How's that?'

"The first one explains, 'If you hit it into the sand, it beeps. If you hit it into the water, it floats. If you play ball at night, it glows.'

" 'Wow,' says his buddy. 'Where did you get it?'

"The first man beamed proudly, 'Found it in the woods.' " Groans and chuckling followed that unexpected punch line, followed by the sounds of people enjoying good food and companionship.

"I'm sure," Gracie changed the subject, "that our Mr. Gravino knows a lot more than he's letting on."

"We all do," Uncle Miltie said, adding humorously, "and that's not even thinking about the part we forgot."

"I mean, *about* the people and animals getting sick, the sheep dying. All of that.

He's been investigating it all along. But why hasn't he so much as mentioned what he's found?"

Lester advised, "Just ask him."

"I did. He didn't answer me straight."

"That's Rocky," Don reminded her. "About what you'd expect from a dog person."

"Now that I think about it, I remember him saying that the vet gave us a reduced rate when treating the cocker spaniel. He even knew how much. How did he know that?"

"What are you saying, Gracie?" Lester asked.

"I don't know. What's out around Coltrain?"

"Hills. Cows." Even Uncle Miltie knew that.

"Why Coltrain? It's way out on the county line."

"Rocky asked me specifically about Coltrain. Let's see. He asked me if Dale Springer, the factory rep, had taken me out that way."

And Roy Bell, too, had been touting the advantages of Coltrain. What's more, Roy seemed to be going pretty far out of his way to do her a favor just now. Did he really have a hole in his schedule, or was he trying to butter her up? Up until this week, Gracie would have said he never had a schedule to have a hole in, anyway. He worked when he felt like it, doing what he felt like doing.

Something very peculiar was going on here, Gracie was certain. But she could not quite put her finger on it.

They soon finished lunch with no further mention of the proposed factory or even of any mysterious ailments.

Woof woof woof! Howooooor!

"Look!" Gracie pointed across the lot, as she and her uncle were headed to her car. "There are Rover and Gent!"

"Pretty cute, the way they stick up." Uncle Miltie admired the canine ventilation system.

Gracie, meanwhile, had crossed to greet the noisy pair. Gent and Rover barked approval. The dogs were standing on their hind legs on the front seat, their heads through the partially open sunroof. And on the passenger seat floor was a bundle of printouts. Were these the ones Dr. Wilkins had given Rocky?

"I wonder if it's locked." Gracie tried the door handle.

"It doesn't have to be," Uncle Miltie answered. "When you got two dogs on alert, you don't need to."

But Gracie was already sitting on the seat with her feet on the ground. Instantly, Gent dropped down and began licking her face. Rover tried for her lap. She was going to have to escape being loved to pieces. She shoved them both aside long enough to scoop up the printouts, keeping them from following her out of the car, but only barely.

She shut the door again. Instantly, both heads popped out the sunroof.

"Look!" She wanted to spread the sheets out across but it was still drizzling. The footers told her that these were indeed Dr. Wilkins's printouts. One listed various maladies of sheep. Another reviewed natural plant toxins known to affect sheep. And the third interested Gracie most of all. It was titled, "Quick-acting Poisons."

32

Gracie was no fan of the frequently combative Willow Bend town council meetings. She'd found them maddening even when she'd served with El as the recording secretary for a couple of terms.

And in all the intervening years, she hadn't experienced much change of heart.

On this occasion, she sat between Pastor Paul and Dale Springer, awaiting her turn at the podium. People were still jamming into the high school gym. The bleachers down front had filled up twenty minutes earlier. Now the risers in back were getting crowded, as well. It was going to be a full house.

The mayor, Tom Ritter, called the meeting to order around ten minutes past the scheduled time, and still the crowd was slow to grow quiet. Finally, there was a brief lull, and Tom seized the moment to bang his gavel, demanding attention.

Gracie knew the drill. Minutes, treasurer's report, old business, new business. She'd seen the agenda when they arrived; the controversial factory was the only new business.

Marge sat in the front row crocheting. She caught Gracie's eye and waved. Moral support. Gracie then noted Jessica Larson and her husband in the front row. There sat Harry Durant, too, jaw clenched and arms crossed. Beside Harry sat Roy Bell.

Before she realized it, Gracie was watching Dale Springer step up to the podium. Dale attached a mobile mike to her collar and walked over to a laptop computer on a stand. The house lights dimmed.

"Interesting." Paul Meyer leaned over to Gracie. "PowerPoint."

"What's PowerPoint?"

"A fancy computerized presentation. Watch."

On the side wall, Dale displayed a giant image of Frank Billingsly's sheep pasture. The photo was ten feet tall at least. As she described what her company had in mind, Dale superimposed an architectural representation of the factory itself and of the parking area across the creek, as well as the channelized stream that so haunted Gracie. She described the benefits to come in glowing terms, with full-color pie charts and bar graphs. Before she was through, Gracie was totally convinced that this new business was either the area's ticket out of poverty into the wonderful world of luxury — or else the biggest scam ever foisted on the county.

The lights came up.

Dale looked around the room with an infectious air of confidence. "I'm sure there are questions."

"I have two." From around the third row, Rocky Gravino stood up. "Ms. Springer, did you or an agent acting for you poison Frank Billingsly's sheep?"

She never batted an eye. "I did not. I have no idea who did, so I cannot answer further."

"The other question: Who's paying you to stay away from Coltrain?"

"No one!" She glared, instantly indignant. "We're considering five sites based on accessibility, proximity of a potential workforce, and ability to provide utilities cheaply. As for —"

The editor raised his voice. "The same freeway that goes through here goes through Coltrain. They're closer to utilities, and people from Willow Bend who want to work in Coltrain can get there in twenty minutes. Moreover, landowners in that area are more than ready to deal. Roy Bell here, for instance, is one of them. He approached you, asking you to consider a property he owns near Coltrain. You demurred.

"Ms. Springer, a friend and I went out driving around yesterday afternoon, after lunch. I left my car in the lot, and he and I explored the logical options you seem to have forgotten about. I'm suggesting two things. One, Frank's place is *not* your first choice. It simply makes a good smokescreen while you set up a deal for a different property. With everyone focusing on the Billingsly land, it leaves you to play your games unscrutinized. And the best way to set up that smokescreen was to kill off a couple sheep.

"Two, unbeknownst to your bosses you have been accepting bribes under the table to consider certain properties and disregard other, equally viable ones. I have an exact list of those properties you've picked out as well as those you've refused to consider. It will appear in tomorrow's paper."

She looked daggers at him. He merely smiled.

"I have it all fully documented. Thank you, Ms. Springer, Mayor." Rocky sat down, still grinning.

Dale Springer started to say something,

but Roy Bell drowned her out. "He's right! And I'll swear on a stack of *Farmer's Almanacs* that he's right! I refused to play her game, and I don't have her kind of cash."

"You're out of order," Mayor Ritter told him. "You're not on the list to speak!" He pounded on the podium with his gavel. Nothing happened.

And then Pastor Paul stood up. "Blessed are the peacemakers." He marched over to the mayor's chair. Leaning forward, he conferred at length with the gavel-wielder.

Paul then led Dale Springer back over to her laptop at the side of the room. She typed away on it a moment.

The room went black.

Gracie gasped in tandem with the entire room. She knew the silence that suddenly fell would last only a few seconds. The sole illumination was issuing from the exit signs over the doors. The effect was definitely eerie.

Pastor Paul's voice, young and strong, suddenly boomed, "Lord in Heaven, we ask your blessing on this congregation here gathered."

The lights came up slowly. Paul stood alone, his hands raised in the manner of the worshippers at Waxmire Tabernacle. "We thank You for the bounty You provide and look to You for wisdom as we make decisions. Amen!"

He crossed to the podium. "Ladies and gentlemen, I am the friend who went with Rocco Gravino yesterday. Now, those of you who know us are well aware that we rarely see eye to eye. But yesterday, as we explored the places Dale Springer never mentioned, we found ourselves agreeing on several important issues.

"First and foremost, we here in this huge and magnificent country can no longer simply bulldoze and build wherever we wish. Gradually, there will no longer be enough wild places to allow that luxury. The key, then, to the best location must be 'environmental wisdom.' What is the wisest choice for altering the least amount of natural land?"

Dale Springer took her seat beside Gracie. "What's his angle, anyway? Who's he fronting for?"

Gracie felt serene, at last. "God," she gently replied.

"Also, first and foremost," the pastor continued, "we must look to and consider all people. Harry, how many do you employ full-time?"

Harry Durant, startled at being singled out, fumbled at first. "Three, full-time.

Part-time, a couple more, depending."

"Roy?"

"One or two part-time is all."

Pastor Paul nodded. "I submit to you that Harry's five or six are neither more nor less important than Roy's one or two part-timers or the proposed factory's two hundred. We can afford to look after every single neighbor. We must do it."

"He's going to ruin my deal," Dale muttered under her breath. "I just know it."

"There's another factor we haven't considered." Pastor Paul looked around. "Tourism. People stop in to look at significant and innovative things. If the proposed factory is a model of environmentally wise use of natural resources, it will attract visitors who will want to observe it. There will be those, I think, too, who'll want to use it as a basis for their own projects. And if its design is attractive and environmentally appropriate, as well, it will draw visitors on that basis. As Cordelia Fountain, and Abe Wasserman, and many others among you know, visitors take pictures and leave money. The more we attract, the healthier the economy, but with minimal cost to our present lifestyle."

The pastor addressed Mayor Ritter. "May I suggest that you resolve to consider all proposed sites within a thirty-mile radius, with conservation of habitat and tourism given equal consideration with jobs and convenience."

The mayor asked, "Do I hear a proposal?"

Ann O'Neill raised her hand. "I so propose."

"Second?"

"I second!" Ruth Stefano, another councilwoman, jumped right in.

"In favor? Opposed? Passed! Further comment?" The mayor looked around.

Pastor Paul returned to his seat beside Gracie, leaning around her to see Dale Springer better. "Dale, you have two ways to go here. When the paper comes out in the morning, you're going to look foolish. You accepted favors and you got caught. You'll probably never be prosecuted, but your chance to exert influence here is finished. You can go back to your bosses and say, 'Find somewhere else. That area can't sustain our operation.'

"Or you can take the high road. Start the search over again and do it right this time. Work with us as partners instead of trying to take advantage of us. It's up to you."

She studied him for several seconds, started to say something, then didn't. She slowly and carefully picked up her computer and her materials and, keeping as much dignity as she could muster, strode out of the gym.

Gracie regarded Paul. "Poor Roger," she said, sighing. Then she asked him, "Remember sitting in my kitchen a couple days ago? I have an answer for you now. I happened to see you talking to Chuckie Moon in the school lot. The phone book. Nice and direct! Or nice and directory, if you prefer. It was an effective solution.

"And look what you did just now! The whole place was coming apart, and you brought it back together.

"Paul, God doesn't use a person because he or she is a particular kind of person. He uses us because we're willing to be used. You make yourself available to God. You seem to think that your weakness is your youth, but, actually, you have a great advantage because you *know* your weakness. Most don't. Not only that, you'll outgrow it. So don't you dare think about resigning! We need exactly who you are, not what you wish you were. Understood?"

"Understood."

Only one very big puzzle remained. Who had been poisoning the land? And what had happened to Gooseberry? Tomorrow she would tackle Rocky. She still really wanted to know about those sheep!

33

The kitchen TV was blasting out commercials interspersed with tiny dollops of the morning news. Uncle Miltie munched away, oblivious. In the middle of the kitchen floor, Gooseberry thrust a hind leg straight up in the air and started giving himself a vigorous bath. As she tackled her own bowl of cereal, Gracie began to strategize the menu for the high school principal's upcoming event. In short, all was as usual for a weekday morning.

Except for a funny scratching noise. What was it?

Gracie abandoned her cereal and stepped outside onto the back stoop.

Roy Bell, his toolbox open beside him, knelt head down at the corner of her house. With a trowel he was digging dirt away from the foundation. "Okay," he ordered, "now dig out the rest." He paused. "Much water?"

"Naw," came a disinterested voice from around the corner. The scratching recommenced on the other side of the house.

"Good morning, Roy."

He looked up at her and the biggest grin split his wiry little face. "Gracie!" He clambered to his feet. "I was afraid I might wake you, so I didn't ring your doorbell."

"Besides, there's the cat. I know. So how's this project coming? It turned out to be more work than expected, it seems."

"Yeah, a few little things cropped up. Say! That pastor of yours is a gem. He and Rocky. When the Springer woman told me it'd be a cold day in hell before she'd consider my parcel down by Coltrain, I figured something was up, but I couldn't prove anything. Now here they are, giving it a chance again."

"I'm glad it's turning out for you."

"Mr. Bell? Is this deep enough?" A shock of green hair appeared around the corner.

"Good morning, Chuckie." Gracie gave him a smile.

He acknowledged her in barely audible tones.

"No school today?"

He muttered something else.

Roy looked at him. "Say it louder. She can't hear you when you mumble like that."

"Three-day suspension."

Roy shot a cursory glance at Chuckie and

at the hole he had just dug. "I'm gonna mix the mortar. Be ready to rock and roll in a minute here." He pulled the cord on his little cement mixer. The lawnmower-sized motor coughed and roared.

Chuckie scooped a shovel of sand and tossed it into the barrel.

Gracie went back inside. She pretended she was working on the catering job, but she couldn't, really. She was working, instead, on the problem of who'd stink-bombed her church. She felt she had to know, and that finally answers were starting to form.

Uncle Miltie finally zapped the TV off and launched himself toward the front door. "Gotta see if the town is still standing."

Roughly translated, that meant, "Let's go find out if my buddies gathered at the senior center are up for a hand of pinochle."

As far as Gracie was concerned, it was time for a plan.

Into a bowl she scooped about a cup of flour and maybe half a cup or so of sugar. Baking powder in the usual amount, a teaspoon or a little more. She added several tablespoons of butter-flavored oil and beat in enough milk to make a smooth, stiff batter.

She emptied a can of cherry pie filling into a brownie pan, poured the batter over the top, and popped it in the oven. While it baked for half an hour, she mixed up a punch of half and half cranberry-apple juice and lemon-lime soda. As a finishing touch, she closed Gooseberry up in her bedroom.

She walked outside and checked on the workers. Stripped to the waist, the two masons were struggling mightily with a footing.

"Roy? Fresh cobbler and punch. Can you and Chuckie break a few minutes?"

"Where's the cat?"

"Safely locked up."

"Five minutes."

It was more like three minutes. The erstwhile laborers, T-shirts hastily pulled on, stomped inside and settled at her kitchen table.

Roy enumerated the virtues of Pastor Paul some more, and Gracie invited him to church yet again. The conversation drifted around. Chuckie accepted a second piece of cobbler.

Then Gracie asked, "Chuckie, I understand that Jeffrey is getting the glory, but that, actually, you're the chemistry whiz."

Obviously, he hadn't been expecting that. "Yeah, you might say that."

Roy looked curious. "A chemistry whiz on a three-day suspension?"

"That was something else. Didn't have anything to do with chemistry." He glanced for a moment at Gracie and returned his full attention to his cobbler.

"Tell me something. In your chemistry classes, have you ever learned how to make a potato taste like a banana?"

"Sure." Chuckie finished off his cobbler and washed it down with a swallow of punch. "We got that in organic. Every flavor is really just chemicals, you know. Food's only chemicals. These people who say 'natural foods' are really saying 'natural chemicals.' And when thcy say 'no chemicals,' they're really saying 'no extra chemicals in your chemicals.' Did you know that?"

"Fascinating."

"Anyway, some of the flavors, like banana, are really just simple salts. So you can make them in the school lab. Add the right hydroxyl to the right acid and you get these flavors. Banana is one of the easiest."

"I thought that if you added a hydroxyl to an acid you got hydrogen sulfide."

"No, that's another kind of thing. Stink bomb."

"Come on." Roy stood up and jabbed Chuckie's arm. "We gotta make these banana-flavored footings."

Gracie asked, "May I send him out in a few minutes? I have another question."

"Sure. Go ahead." Roy left.

Chuckie watched him go out the door. He suddenly looked very eager to go back to work.

"Why are you spying on me?" she asked.

"I'm not."

"Yes, you are. I see you up on the corner, watching, every now and then. Will you please tell me why?"

Chuckie looked at his hands. He looked at the tablecloth. He looked at his empty plate. He looked just about everywhere you could see by gazing downward. Would he crack?

He did. "I don't know."

Gracie said nothing.

Chuckie went on. "I want to make the girls like me, you know? But nothing I do is the right thing. Then one day I saw Mr. Gravino stop by. And he opened the car door for you. You and he get along so comfortable, but you're a man and a woman. I want to be able to be that way with girls, and I can't. I keep watching your place, wishing I could get along with guys, girls, everybody, like you do."

"Why won't they let you?"

Chuckie looked at her. "It's me. It's not them."

Should Gracie mention Angie Billingsly and her feeling that Chuckie frightened her? "I also happen to know about a certain person who can rip a phone book in two. Do you remember how frightened you were?" Gracie raised a hand. "And rightly so. He's dangerous. That's how you often make others feel. Did you like being around him?"

Chuckie didn't reply, but Gracie knew he saw the point.

"In the same way, people are often afraid to hang around you too." She laid a hand on his arm and he did not pull away. "I have no idea about your home life, but I suspect it's been difficult. You're angry and frustrated. But that won't win friends. Being a friend will."

"I don't know how."

"It's one of the oldest rules going and still one of the best. Do unto others as you wish they would do to you."

Chuckie grinned suddenly. "Here I thought that was 'Do unto others before they do unto you.' "

Gracie laughed. She sat back. "Good luck in life, Chuckie! I'm sure you'll do well."

He mumbled something, but this time it wasn't a hostile mumble. He put his plate in the sink and went outside.

Chuckie was not the perpetrator of the stink bombs, and probably not of the pollutants, either. She must confront someone else.

34

Gracie walked into the high school and headed to the office. It was so quiet. No one spoke, no one shouted.

No lockers clanged, no doors slammed. School was still twenty minutes short of letting out.

She signed in and gave Bud Smith her proposed menu. They discussed cost for a few minutes. Then they went down to Room 36 and waited.

The hall bell clanged, and a racetrack announcer might as well have yelled, "They're off!"

The door to Room 36 burst open. The boys who always must be first out came plunging through. When they saw their principal standing there, they instantly adopted a more sedate demeanor.

"Jeffrey? Wait." Gracie fixed her most no-nonsense gaze on the child in the doorway just at that moment.

Jeffrey looked at Gracie and his principal

and shrugged. He stood aside as the rest of the children left. Gracie and Bud went into the room.

"Sit." Bud pointed to a desk.

Jeffrey sat.

Gracie pulled a chair-desk around and sat in front of him and Bud sat beside him.

He looked worried. "What?"

Gracie began. "It's very easy to make banana flavoring. The chemicals you need are right here in this school's laboratory." She waited a moment. "And it's just as easy to make a stink bomb." She waited another long moment.

Jeffrey started to squirm a little.

"I understand you would see it as a prank when you ruined that bowl of potato salad at the youth group supper, but why did you stink-bomb our church?"

"I never did that!"

Gracie said quietly, not as an argument but as a statement, "Yes, you did."

Jeffrey looked at Bud Smith. He stared back. He looked at Gracie. She watched his face.

He licked his lips. His expression was easy to read. You could almost tell when he mentally mounted a defense and then demolished it, and tried another.

Finally, he just gave up. "Why not? It wasn't Sunday."

"Why the police station?"

He shrugged. "Hey, look, like you said, it was a joke. It was just so cool to watch the cops come running out like that. And the people at the church. No big deal."

"Harm? Let's talk about potato salad."

"It was Chuckie! He did it and told you it was us."

"No. It could have been. But Chuckie wasn't at the supper that night. You were. *You* put the banana flavoring in the potato salad."

"Roger did it too."

"Whether Roger was in on it is not at issue. We're looking at your guilt. When you make these things, there are leftovers, right? Chemicals you can't use. Waste."

"Sure."

"And you dump them in Willow Reach. The creek by Frank Billingsly's."

"Roger told, that fink!"

"No, Roger didn't. Although I saw him coming back with you one day, so I know you two must have been up to something together."

"We did lots of experiments. Some of them turned out, too. I have this huge chemistry set in the basement."

"You made quite a few animals sick. Some died."

"If we did, it was an accident. We dumped some leftovers and some bum experiments. That's all."

"Why?"

"Why not? Mom said I wasn't allowed to put them down her drain because they stank, so I had to dump them somewhere." He watched her defiantly for a moment. "I can do anything I want to. I'm smart!"

"Yes, you can. I agree completely." Gracie nodded emphatically. "You *can* do whatever you want, and if you get caught, it's probably not illegal. At least, not very."

Jeffrey seemed amazed that someone agreed with him.

Then Gracie added, "But that doesn't mean it's all right. Responsibility is doing what's right when you could just as well do what's wrong. It's refraining from doing something even though you could.

"Responsibility separates good people from bad ones. It separates adults from children."

Bud Smith looked unhappy. "This doesn't come under the school's purview exactly — a home chemistry lab — but close enough. I'll arrange a conference with his parents."

"No!" Jeffrey looked terrified. "I'll quit, I promise. No more. I'll get rid of all the chemicals."

"Too late."

Gracie stood up. "I'll talk to you later this evening, Bud. Blessings."

The halls had nearly cleared. Only a few students, mostly boy-girl combinations, lingered at the lockers. She walked out through the main doors into cloudy weather.

There on the pavement was today's paper, probably left by a student. Gracie picked it up.

Rocky's exposé covered the front section. She noted with satisfaction that Pastor Paul's role in uncovering the truth was well displayed. She would read it in detail when she got home. But it wasn't what she was looking for now. She leafed through the ads, every page. Nothing.

So Rocky hadn't put that ad in the paper yet. If he didn't watch it, he'd be a two-dog owner. Maybe he was already.

Maybe she would stop by the *Gazette* office and address him directly on this issue. Even invite him to dinner and get the full scoop.

It was something to look forward to, Gracie knew that for sure. But, in the meantime, Gooseberry was probably wondering where she was.

Zesty Potato Salad

✓ 6–8 medium Yukon Gold potatoes with jackets (other potatoes also work)
✓ ½–¾ cup sweet pickle juice (or vinegar)
✓ 3–4 scallions, diced
✓ 3 ribs celery, diced
✓ ¼ cup green pepper, diced
✓ 2 hardboiled eggs, diced
✓ 2–3 tablespoons mayonnaise
✓ ¼ cup pimiento
✓ salt & pepper to taste
✓ dill weed (optional)
✓ tomatoes and radishes (garnish)

Boil potatoes until cooked (20-35 minutes, depending on size). Keep in their skins and slice for the salad. While still warm, add pickle juice or vinegar so potatoes will absorb the liquid.

When cooled, add additional ingredients. Add mayonnaise to desired creaminess — you may want more than called for. Chill and serve. You can add tomatoes and radishes for garnish.

About the Author

Not unlike Bizet's title character Carmen, SANDY DENGLER leads an interesting double life. By day she is a mild-mannered free-lance writer. By night, she builds dinosaurs and other paleo beasts for Oklahoma's new natural history museum. In between, she enjoys her hobbies of working on a variety of needlework and painting projects. Born in Ohio, she earned a bachelor's degree in zoology at Bowling Green State University and a master's degree in desert ecology at Arizona State University in Tempe. Bill, whom she met in graduate school and married in 1963, became a career National Park Service ranger, and they raised their two daughters, Alyce and Mary, in such exotic places as Death Valley, Yosemite, Mount Rainier and Acadia. The daughters, with their families, now live in the Puget Sound area of Washington State.

As a child, Sandy dreamt of becoming a paleontologist. But little farm girls in rural Ohio in the 1940s and 1950s didn't even think about earning a doctorate in a man's profession. Fifty years later, with her husband's encouragement, she is pursuing that dream. She has commenced study at the University of Oklahoma with an eye toward a Ph.D. in paleontology.

She and Bill reside in Norman, Oklahoma.

The employees of Thorndike Press hope you have enjoyed this Large Print book. All our Thorndike and Wheeler Large Print titles are designed for easy reading, and all our books are made to last. Other Thorndike Press Large Print books are available at your library, through selected bookstores, or directly from us.

For information about titles, please call:
   (800) 223-1244
or visit our Web site at:
   www.gale.com/thorndike
   www.gale.com/wheeler

To share your comments, please write:

   Publisher
   Thorndike Press
   295 Kennedy Memorial Drive
   Waterville, ME 04901

Guideposts magazine and the Daily Guideposts annual devotion book are available in large-print format by contacting:
   Guideposts Customer Service
   39 Seminary Hill Road
   Carmel, NY 10512
   or
   www. guideposts.com

KIc f